The Wandering Jew (Volume

Eugène Sue

Alpha Editions

This edition published in 2024

ISBN 9789362993069

Design and Setting By
Alpha Editions
www.alphaedis.com
Email - info@alphaedis.com

As per information held with us this book is in Public Domain.
This book is a reproduction of an important historical work.
Alpha Editions uses the best technology to reproduce historical work
in the same manner it was first published to preserve its original nature.
Any marks or number seen are left intentionally to preserve.

Contents

BOOK IX.	- 1 -
CHAPTER XV.	- 2 -
CHAPTER XVI.	- 6 -
CHAPTER XVII.	- 14 -
CHAPTER XVIII.	- 25 -
CHAPTER XIX.	- 34 -
CHAPTER XX.	- 38 -
CHAPTER XXI.	- 44 -
CHAPTER XXIL	- 49 -
CHAPTER XXIII.	- 55 -
CHAPTER XXIV.	- 62 -
CHAPTER XXV.	- 67 -
CHAPTER XXVI.	- 74 -
CHAPTER XXVII.	- 82 -
CHAPTER XXVIII.	- 88 -
CHAPTER XXIX.	- 94 -
CHAPTER XXX.	- 100 -
CHAPTER XXXI.	- 105 -
CHAPTER XXXII.	- 112 -

BOOK IX.

CHAPTER XV.

THE CONSTANT WANDERER.

It is night. The moon shines and the stars glimmer in the midst of a serene but cheerless sky; the sharp whistlings of the north wind, that fatal, dry, and icy breeze, ever and anon burst forth in violent gusts. With its harsh and cutting breath, it sweeps Montmartre's Heights. On the highest point of the hills, a man is standing. His long shadow is cast upon the stony, moon-lit ground. He gazes on the immense city, which lies outspread beneath his feet. PARIS—with the dark outline of its towers, cupolas, domes, and steeples, standing out from the limpid blue of the horizon, while from the midst of the ocean of masonry, rises a luminous vapor, that reddens the starry azure of the sky. It is the distant reflection of the thousand fires, which at night, the hour of pleasures, light up so joyously the noisy capital.

"No," said the wayfarer; "it is not to be. The Lord will not exact it. Is not twice enough?

"Five centuries ago, the avenging hand of the Almighty drove me hither from the uttermost confines of Asia. A solitary traveller, I had left behind me more grief, despair, disaster, and death, than the innumerable armies of a hundred devastating conquerors. I entered this town, and it too was decimated.

"Again, two centuries ago, the inexorable hand, which leads me through the world, brought me once more hither; and then, as the time before, the plague, which the Almighty attaches to my steps, again ravaged this city, and fell first on my brethren, already worn out with labor and misery.

"My brethren—mine?—the cobbler of Jerusalem, the artisan accursed by the Lord, who, in my person, condemned the whole race of workmen, ever suffering, ever disinherited, ever in slavery, toiling on like me without rest or pause, without recompense or hope, till men, women, and children, young and old, all die beneath the same iron yoke—that murderous yoke, which others take in their turn, thus to be borne from age to age on the submissive and bruised shoulders of the masses.

"And now, for the third time in five centuries, I reach the summit of one of the hills that overlook the city. And perhaps I again bring with me fear, desolation, and death.

"Yet this city, intoxicated with the sounds of its joys and its nocturnal revelries, does not know—oh! does not know that I am at its gates.

"But no, no! my presence will not be a new calamity. The Lord, in his impenetrable views, has hitherto led me through France, so as to avoid the humblest hamlet; and the sound of the funeral knell has not accompanied my passage.

"And, moreover, the spectre has left me—the green, livid spectre, with its hollow, bloodshot eyes. When I touched the soil of France, its damp and icy hands was no longer clasped in mine—and it disappeared.

"And yet—I feel that the atmosphere of death is around me.

"The sharp whistlings of that fatal wind cease not, which, catching me in their whirl, seem to propagate blasting and mildew as they blow.

"But perhaps the wrath of the Lord is appeased, and my presence here is only a threat—to be communicated in some way to those whom it should intimidate.

"Yes; for otherwise he would smite with a fearful blow, by first scattering terror and death here in the heart of the country, in the bosom of this immense city!

"Oh! no, no! the Lord will be merciful. No! he will not condemn me to this new torture.

"Alas! in this city, my brethren are more numerous and miserable than elsewhere. And should I be their messenger of death?"

"No! the Lord will have pity. For, alas! the seven descendants of my sister have at length met in this town. And to them likewise should I be the messenger of death, instead of the help they so much need?

"For that woman, who like me wanders from one border of the earth to the other, after having once more rent asunder the nets of their enemies, has gone forth upon her endless journey.

"In vain she foresaw that new misfortunes threatened my sister's family. The invisible hand, that drives me on, drives her on also.

"Carried away, as of old, by the irresistible whirlwind, at the moment of leaving my kindred to their fate, she in vain cried with supplicating tone: 'Let me at least, O Lord, complete my task!'—'GO ON!—'A few days, in mercy, only a few poor days!'—'GO ON'—'I leave those I love on the brink of the abyss!'—'GO ON! GO ON!'

"And the wandering star—again started on its eternal round. And her voice, passing through space, called me to the assistance of mine own.

"When that voice readied me, I knew that the descendants of my sister were still exposed to frightful perils. Those perils are even now on the increase.

"Tell me, O Lord! will they escape the scourge, which for so many centuries has weighed down our race?

"Wilt thou pardon me in them? wilt thou punish me in them? Oh, that they might obey the last will of their ancestor!

"Oh, that they might join together their charitable hearts, their valor and their strength, their noble intelligence, and their great riches!

"They would then labor for the future happiness of humanity—they would thus, perhaps, redeem me from my eternal punishment!

"The words of the Son of Man, LOVE YE ONE ANOTHER, will be their only end, their only means.

"By the help of those all-powerful words, they will fight and conquer the false priests, who have renounced the precepts of love, peace, and hope, for lessons of hatred, violence, and despair.

"Those false priests, who, kept in pay by the powerful and happy of this world, their accomplices in every age, instead of asking here below for some slight share of well-being for my unfortunate brethren, dare in thy name, O Lord God, to assert that the poor are condemned to endless suffering in this world—and that the desire or the hope to suffer less is a crime in thine eyes—because the happiness of the few, and the misery of nearly the whole human race, is (O blasphemy!) according to thy will. Is not the very contrary of those murderous words alone worthy of divinity!

"In mercy, hear me, Lord! Rescue from their enemies the descendants of my sister—the artisan as the king's son. Do not let them destroy the germ of so mighty and fruitful an association, which, with thy blessing, would make an epoch in the annals of human happiness!

"Let me unite them, O Lord, since others would divide them—defend them, since others attack; let me give hope to those who have ceased to hope, courage to those who are brought low with fear—let me raise up the falling, and sustain those who persevere in the way of the righteous!

"And, peradventure, their struggles, devotion, virtue, and grief, may expiate my fault—that of a man, whom misfortune alone rendered unjust and wicked.

"Oh! since Thy Almighty hand hath led me hither—to what end I know not—lay aside Thy wrath, I beseech Thee—let me be no longer the instrument of Thy vengeance!

"Enough of woe upon the earth! for the last two years, Thy creatures have fallen by thousands upon my track. The world is decimated. A veil of mourning extends over all the globe.

"From Asia to the icy Pole, they died upon the path of the wanderer. Dost Thou not hear the long-drawn sigh that rises from the earth unto Thee, O Lord?

"Mercy for all! mercy for me!—Let me but unite the descendants of my sister for a single day, and they will be saved!"

As he pronounced these words, the wayfarer sank upon his knees, and raised to heaven, his supplicating hands. Suddenly, the wind blew with redoubled violence; its sharp whistlings were changed into the roar of a tempest.

The traveller shuddered; in a voice of terror he exclaimed: "The blast of death rises in its fury—the whirlwind carries me on—Lord! Thou art then deaf to my prayer?"

"The spectre! oh, the spectre! it is again here! its green face twitching with convulsive spasms—its red eyes rolling in their orbits. Begone! begone!—its hand, oh! its icy hand has again laid hold of mine. Have mercy, heaven!"

"GO ON!"

"Oh, Lord! the pestilence—the terrible plague—must I carry it into this city?—And my brethren will perish the first—they, who are so sorely smitten even now! Mercy!"

"GO ON!"

"And the descendants of my sister. Mercy! Mercy!"

"GO ON!"

"Oh, Lord, have pity!—I can no longer keep my ground; the spectre drags me to the slope of the hill; my walk is rapid as the deadly blast that rages behind me; already do I behold the city gates. Have mercy, Lord, on the descendants of my sister! Spare them; do not make me their executioner; let them triumph over their enemies!"

"GO ON! GO ON!"

"The ground flies beneath my feet; there is the city gate. Lord, it is yet time! Oh, mercy for that sleeping town! Let it not waken to cries of terror, despair, and death! Lord, I am on the threshold. Must it be?—Yes, it is done. Paris, the plague is in thy bosom. The curse—oh, the eternal curse!"

"GO ON! GO ON! GO ON!"

CHAPTER XVI.

THE LUNCHEON.

The morning after the doomed traveller, descending the heights of Montmartre, had entered the walls of Paris, great activity reigned in St. Dizier House. Though it was hardly noon, the Princess de St. Dizier, without being exactly in full dress (she had too much taste for that), was yet arrayed with more care than usual. Her light hair, instead of being merely banded, was arranged in two bunches of curls, which suited very well with her full and florid cheeks. Her cap was trimmed with bright rose-colored ribbon, and whoever had seen the lady in her tight fitting dress of gray-watered silk would have easily guessed that Mrs. Grivois, her tirewoman, must have required the assistance and the efforts of another of the princess's women to achieve so remarkable a reduction in the ample figure of their mistress.

We shall explain the edifying cause of this partial return to the vanities of the world. The princess, attended by Mrs. Grivois, who acted as housekeeper, was giving her final orders with regard to some preparations that were going on in a vast parlor. In the midst of this room was a large round table, covered with crimson velvet, and near it stood several chairs, amongst which, in the place of honor, was an arm chair of gilded wood. In one corner, not far from the chimney, in which burned an excellent fire, was a buffet. On it were the divers materials for a most dainty and exquisite collation. Upon silver dishes were piled pyramids of sandwiches composed of the roes of carp and anchovy paste, with slices of pickled tunny-fish and Lenigord truffles (it was in Lent); on silver dishes, placed over burning spirits of wine, so as to keep them very hot, tails of Meuse crawfish boiled in cream, smoked in golden colored pastry, and seemed to challenge comparison with delicious little Marennes oyster-patties, stewed in Madeira, and flavored with a seasoning of spiced sturgeon. By the side of these substantial dishes were some of a lighter character, such as pineapple tarts, strawberry-creams (it was early for such fruit), and orange-jelly served in the peel, which had been artistically emptied for that purpose. Bordeaux, Madeira, and Alicant sparkled like rubies and topazes in large glass decanters, while two Sevres ewers were filled, one with coffee a la creme, the other with vanilla chocolate, almost in the state of sherbet, from being plunged in a large cooler of chiselled silver, containing ice.

But what gave to this dainty collation a singularly apostolic and papal character were sundry symbols of religious worship carefully represented.

Thus there were charming little Calvaries in apricot paste, sacerdotal mitres in burnt almonds, episcopal croziers in sweet cake, to which the princess added, as a mark of delicate attention, a little cardinal's hat in cherry sweetmeat, ornamented with bands in burnt sugar. The most important, however, of these Catholic delicacies, the masterpiece of the cook, was a superb crucifix in angelica, with a crown of candied berries. These are strange profanations, which scandalize even the least devout. But, from the impudent juggle of the coat of Triers, down to the shameless jest of the shrine at Argenteuil, people, who are pious after the fashion of the princess, seem to take delight in bringing ridicule upon the most respectable traditions.

After glancing with an air of satisfaction at these preparations for the collation, the lady said to Mrs. Grivois, as she pointed to the gilded arm-chair, which seemed destined for the president of the meeting: "Is there a cushion under the table, for his Eminence to rest his feet on? He always complains of cold."

"Yes, your highness," said Mrs. Grivois, when she had looked under the table; "the cushion is there."

"Let also a pewter bottle be filled with boiling water, in case his Eminence should not find the cushion enough to keep his feet warm."

"Yes, my lady."

"And put some more wood on the fire."

"But, my lady, it is already a very furnace. And if his Eminence is always too cold, my lord the Bishop of Halfagen is always too hot. He perspires dreadfully."

The princess shrugged her shoulders, and said to Mrs. Grivois: "Is not his Eminence Cardinal Malipieri the superior of his Lordship the Bishop of Halfagen?"

"Yes, your highness."

"Then, according to the rules of the hierarchy, it is for his Lordship to suffer from the heat, rather than his Eminence from the cold. Therefore, do as I tell you, and put more wood on the fire. Nothing is more natural; his Eminence being an Italian, and his Lordship coming from the north of Belgium, they are accustomed to different temperatures."

"Just as your highness pleases," said Mrs. Grivois, as she placed two enormous logs on the fire; "but in such a heat as there is here his Lordship might really be suffocated."

"I also find it too warm; but does not our holy religion teach us lessons of self-sacrifice and mortification?" said the princess, with a touching expression of devotion.

We have now explained the cause of the rather gay attire of the princess. She was preparing for a reception of prelates, who, along with Father d'Aigrigny and other dignitaries of the Church, had already held at the princely house a sort of council on a small scale. A young bride who gives her first ball, an emancipated minor who gives his first bachelor's dinner, a woman of talent who reads aloud for the first time her first unpublished work, are not more joyous and proud, and, at the same time, more attentive to their guests, than was this lady with her prelates. To behold great interests discussed in her house, and in her presence, to hear men of acknowledged ability ask her advice upon certain practical matters relating to the influence of female congregations, filled the princess with pride, as her claims to consideration were thus sanctioned by Lordships and Eminences, and she took the position, as it were, of a mother of the Church. Therefore, to win these prelates, whether native or foreign, she had recourse to no end of saintly flatteries and sanctified coaxing. Nor could anything be more logical than these successive transfigurations of this heartless woman, who only loved sincerely and passionately the pursuit of intrigue and domination. With the progress of age, she passed naturally from the intrigues of love to those of politics, and from the latter to those of religion.

At the moment she finished inspecting her preparations, the sound of coaches was heard in the courtyard, apprising her of the arrival of the persons she had been expecting. Doubtless, these persons were of the highest rank, for contrary to all custom, she went to receive them at the door of her outer saloon. It was, indeed, Cardinal Malipieri, who was always cold, with the Belgian Bishop of Halfagen, who was always hot. They were accompanied by Father d'Aigrigny. The Roman cardinal was a tall man, rather bony than thin, with a yellowish puffy countenance, haughty and full of craft; he squinted a good deal, and his black eyes were surrounded by a deep brown circle. The Belgian Bishop was short, thick, and fat, with a prominent abdomen, an apoplectic complexion, a slow, deliberate look, and a soft, dimpled, delicate hand.

The company soon assembled in the great saloon. The cardinal instantly crept close to the fire, whilst the bishop, beginning to sweat and blow, cast longing glances at the iced chocolate and coffee, which were to aid him in sustaining the oppressive heat of the artificial dog-day. Father d'Aigrigny, approaching the princess, said to her in a low voice: "Will you give orders for the admittance of Abbe Gabriel de Rennepont, when he arrives?"

"Is that young priest then here?" asked the princess, with extreme surprise.

"Since the day before yesterday. We had him sent for to Paris, by his superiors. You shall know all. As for Father Rodin, let Mrs. Grivois admit him, as the other day, by the little door of the back stairs."

"He will come to-day?"

"He has very important matters to communicate. He desires that both the cardinal and the bishop should be present for they have been informed of everything at Rome by the Superior General, in their quality of associates."

The princess rang the bell, gave the necessary orders, and, returning towards the cardinal, said to him, in a tone of the most earnest solicitude: "Does your Eminence begin to feel a little warmer? Would your Eminence like a bottle of hot water to your feet? Shall we make a larger fire for your Eminence?"

At this proposition, the Belgian bishop, who was wiping the perspiration from his forehead, heaved a despairing sigh.

"A thousand thanks, princess," answered the cardinal to her, in very good French, but with an intolerable Italian accent; "I am really overcome with so much kindness."

"Will not your Lordship take some refreshment?" said the princess to the bishop, as she turned towards the sideboard.

"With your permission, madame, I will take a little iced coffee," said the prelate, making a prudent circuit to approach the dishes without passing before the fire.

"And will not your Eminence try one of these little oyster-patties? They are quite hot," said the princess.

"I know them already, princess," said the cardinal, with the air and look of an epicure; "they are delicious, and I cannot resist the temptation."

"What wine shall I have the honor to offer your Eminence?" resumed the princess, graciously.

"A little claret, if you please, madame;" and as Father d'Aigrigny prepared to fill the cardinal's glass, the princess disputed with him that pleasure.

"Your Eminence will doubtless approve what I have done," said Father d'Aigrigny to the cardinal, whilst the latter was gravely despatching the oyster-patties, "in not summoning for to-day the Bishop of Mogador, the Archbishop of Nanterre, and our holy Mother Perpetue, the lady-superior of St. Mary Convent, the interview we are about to have with his Reverence Father Rodin and Abbe Gabriel being altogether private and confidential."

"Our good father was perfectly right," said the cardinal; "for, though the possible consequences of this Rennepont affair may interest the whole Church, there are some things that are as well kept secret."

"Then I must seize this opportunity to thank your Eminence for having deigned to make an exception in favor of a very obscure and humble servant of the Church," said the princess to the cardinal, with a very deep and respectful curtsey.

"It is only just and right, madame," replied the cardinal, bowing as he replaced his empty glass upon the table; "we know how much the Church is indebted to you for the salutary direction you give to the religious institutions of which you are the patroness."

"With regard to that, your Eminence may be assured that I always refuse assistance to any poor person who cannot produce a certificate from the confessional."

"And it is only thus, madame," resumed the cardinal, this time allowing himself to be tempted by the attractions of the crawfish's tails, "it is only thus that charity has any meaning. I care little that the irreligious should feel hunger, but with the pious it is different;" and the prelate gayly swallowed a mouthful. "Moreover," resumed he, "it is well known with what ardent zeal you pursue the impious, and those who are rebels against the authority of our Holy Father."

"Your Eminence may feel convinced that I am Roman in heart and soul; I see no difference between a Gallican and a Turk," said the princess, bravely.

"The princess is right," said the Belgian bishop: "I will go further, and assert that a Gallican should be more odious to the church than a pagan. In this respect I am of the opinion of Louis XIV. They asked him a favor for a man about the court. 'Never,' said the great king; 'this person is a Jansenist.'—'No, sire; he is an atheist.'—'Oh! that is different; I will grant what he asks,' said the King."

This little episcopal jest made them all laugh. After which Father d'Aigrigny resumed seriously, addressing the cardinal: "Unfortunately, as I was about to observe to your Eminence with regard to the Abbe Gabriel, unless they are very narrowly watched, the lower clergy have a tendency to become infected with dissenting views, and with ideas of rebellion against what they call the despotism of the bishops."

"This young man must be a Catholic Luther!" said the bishop. And, walking on tip-toe, he went to pour himself out a glorious glass of Madeira, in which he soaked some sweet cake, made in the form of a crozier.

Led by his example, the Cardinal, under pretence of warming his feet by drawing still closer to the fire, helped himself to an excellent glass of old Malaga, which he swallowed by mouthfuls, with an air of profound meditation; after which he resumed: "So this Abbe Gabriel starts as a reformer. He must be an ambitious man. Is he dangerous?"

"By our advice his superiors have judged him to be so. They have ordered him to come hither. He will soon be here, and I will tell your Eminence why I have sent for him. But first, I have a note on the dangerous tendencies of the Abbe Gabriel. Certain questions were addressed to him, with regard to some of his acts, and it was in consequence of his answers that his superiors recalled him."

So saying, Father d'Aigrigny, took from his pocket-book a paper, which he read as follows:

"'Question.—Is it true that you performed religious rites for an inhabitant of your parish who died in final impenitence of the most detestable kind, since he had committed suicide?

"'Answer of Abbe Gabriel.—I paid him the last duties, because, more than any one else, because of his guilty end, he required the prayers of the church. During the night which followed his interment I continually implored for him the divine mercy.

"'Q.—Is it true that you refused a set of silver-gilt sacramental vessels, and other ornaments, with which one of the faithful, in pious zeal, wished to endow your parish?

"'A.—I refused the vessels and embellishments, because the house of the Lord should be plain and without ornament, so as to remind the faithful that the divine Saviour was born in a stable. I advised the person who wished to make these useless presents to my parish to employ the money in judicious almsgiving, assuring him it would be more agreeable to the Lord.'"

"What a bitter and violent declamation against the adorning of our temples!" cried the cardinal. "This young priest is most dangerous. Continue, my good father."

And, in his indignation, his Eminence swallowed several mouthfuls of strawberry-cream. Father d'Aigrigny continued.

"'Q.—Is it true that you received in your parsonage, and kept there for some days, an inhabitant of the village, by birth a Swiss, belonging to the Protestant communion? Is it true that not only you did not attempt to convert him to the one Catholic and Apostolic faith, but that you carried so far the neglect of your sacred duties as to inter this heretic in the ground consecrated for the repose of true believers?

"'A.—One of my brethren was houseless. His life had been honest and laborious. In his old age his strength had failed him, and sickness had come at the back of it; almost in a dying state, he had been driven from his humble dwelling by a pitiless landlord, to whom he owed a year's rent. I received the old man in my house, and soothed his last days. The poor creature had toiled and suffered all his life; dying, he uttered no word of bitterness at his hard fate; he recommended his soul to God and piously kissed the crucifix. His pure and simple spirit returned to the bosom of its Creator. I closed his eyes with respect, I buried him, I prayed for him; and, though he died in the Protestant faith, I thought him worthy of a place in consecrated ground.'"

"Worse and worse!" said the cardinal. "This tolerance is monstrous. It is a horrible attack on that maxim of Catholicism: 'Out of the pale of the Church there is no salvation.'"

"And all this is the more serious, my lord," resumed Father d'Aigrigny, "because the mildness, charity, and Christian devotion of Abbe Gabriel have excited, not only in his parish, but in all the surrounding districts, the greatest enthusiasm. The priests of the neighboring parishes have yielded to the general impulse, and it must be confessed that but for his moderation a wide-spread schism would have commenced."

"But what do you hope will result from bringing him here?" said the prelate.

"The position of Abbe Gabriel is complicated; first of all, he is the heir of the Rennepont family."

"But has he not ceded his rights?" asked the cardinal.

"Yes, my lord; and this cession, which was at first informal, has lately, with his free consent, been made perfectly regular in law; for he had sworn, happen what might, to renounce his part of the inheritance in favor of the Society of Jesus. Nevertheless, his Reverence Father Rodin thinks, that if your Eminence, after explaining to Abbe Gabriel that he was about to be recalled by his superiors, were to propose to him some eminent position at Rome, he might be induced to leave France, and we might succeed in arousing within him those sentiments of ambition which are doubtless only sleeping for the present; your Eminence, having observed, very judiciously, that every reformer must be ambitious."

"I approve of this idea," said the cardinal, after a moment's reflection; "with his merit and power of acting on other men, Abbe Gabriel may rise very high, if he is docile; and if he should not be so, it is better for the safety of the Church that he should be at Rome than here—for you know, my good father, we have securities that are unfortunately wanting in France."[36]

After some moments of silence, the cardinal said suddenly to Father d'Aigrigny: "As we were talking of Father Rodin, tell me frankly what you think of him."

"Your Eminence knows his capacity," said Father d'Aigrigny, with a constrained and suspicious air; "our reverend Father-General—"

"Commissioned him to take your place," said the cardinal; "I know that. He told me so at Rome. But what do you think of the character of Father Rodin? Can one have full confidence in him?"

"He has so complete, so original, so secret, and so impenetrable a mind," said Father d'Aigrigny, with hesitation, "that it is difficult to form any certain judgment with respect to him."

"Do you think him ambitious?" said the cardinal, after another moment's pause. "Do you not suppose him capable of having other views than those of the greater glory of his Order?—Come, I have reasons for speaking thus," added the prelate, with emphasis.

"Why," resumed Father d'Aigrigny, not without suspicion, for the game is played cautiously between people of the same craft, "what should your Eminence think of him, either from your own observation, or from the report of the Father-General?"

"I think—that if his apparent devotion to his Order really concealed some after-thought—it would be well to discover it—for, with the influence that he has obtained at Rome (as I have found out), he might one day, and that shortly, become very formidable."

"Well!" cried Father d'Aigrigny, impelled by his jealousy of Rodin; "I am, in this respect, of the same opinion as your Eminence; for I have sometimes perceived in him flashes of ambition, that were as alarming as they were extraordinary—and since I must tell all to your Eminence—"

Father d'Aigrigny was unable to continue; at this moment Mrs. Grivois, who had been knocking at the door, half-opened it, and made a sign to her mistress. The princess answered by bowing her head, and Mrs. Grivois again withdrew. A second afterwards Rodin entered the room.

[36] It is known that, in 1845, the Inquisition, solitary confinement, etc., still existed at Rome.

CHAPTER XVII.

RENDERING THE ACCOUNT.

At sight of Rodin, the two prelates and Father d'Aigrigny rose spontaneously, so much were they overawed by the real superiority of this man; their faces, just before contracted with suspicion and jealousy, suddenly brightened up, and seemed to smile on the reverend father with affectionate deference. The princess advanced some steps to meet him.

Rodin, badly dressed as ever, leaving on the soft carpet the muddy track of his clumsy shoes, put his umbrella into one corner, and advanced towards the table—not with his accustomed humility, but with slow step, uplifted head, and steady glance; not only did he feel himself in the midst of his partisans, but he knew that he could rule them all by the power of his intellect.

"We were speaking of your reverence, my dear, good father," said the cardinal, with charming affability.

"Ah!" said Rodin, looking fixedly at the prelate; "and what were you saying?"

"Why," replied the Belgian bishop, wiping his forehead, "all the good that can be said of your reverence."

"Will you not take something, my good father?" said the princess to Rodin, as she pointed to the splendid sideboard.

"Thank you, madame, I have eaten my radish already this morning."

"My secretary, Abbe Berlini, who was present at your repast, was, indeed, much astonished at your reverence's frugality," said the prelate: "it is worthy of an anchorite."

"Suppose we talk of business," said Rodin, abruptly, like a man accustomed to lead and control the discussion.

"We shall always be most happy to hear you," said the prelate. "Your reverence yourself fixed to-day to talk over this great Rennepont affair. It is of such importance, that it was partly the cause of my journey to France; for to support the interests of the glorious Company of Jesus, with which I have the honor of being associated, is to support the interests of Rome itself, and I promised the reverend Father-General that I would place myself entirely at your orders."

"I can only repeat what his Eminence has just said," added the bishop. "We set out from Rome together, and our ideas are just the same."

"Certainly," said Rodin, addressing the cardinal, "your Eminence may serve our cause, and that materially. I will tell you how presently."

Then, addressing the princess, he continued: "I have desired Dr. Baleinier to come here, madame, for it will be well to inform him of certain things."

"He will be admitted as usual," said the princess.

Since Rodin's arrival Father d'Aigrigny had remained silent; he seemed occupied with bitter thoughts, and with some violent internal struggle. At last, half rising, he said to the prelate, in a forced tone of voice: "I will not ask your Eminence to judge between the reverend Father Rodin and myself. Our General has pronounced, and I have obeyed. But, as your Eminence will soon see our superior, I should wish that you would grant me the favor to report faithfully the answers of Father Rodin to one or two questions I am about to put to him."

The prelate bowed. Rodin looked at Father d'Aigrigny with an air of surprise, and said to him, dryly: "The thing is decided. What is the use of questions?"

"Not to justify myself," answered Father d'Aigrigny, "but to place matters in their true light before his Eminence."

"Speak, then; but let us have no useless speeches," said Rodin, drawing out his large silver watch, and looking at it. "By two o'clock I must be at Saint-Sulpice."

"I will be as brief as possible," said Father d'Aigrigny, with repressed resentment. Then, addressing Rodin, he resumed: "When your reverence thought fit to take my place, and to blame, very severely perhaps, the manner in which I had managed the interests confided to my care, I confess honestly that these interests were gravely compromised."

"Compromised?" said Rodin, ironically; "you mean lost. Did you not order me to write to Rome, to bid them renounce all hope?"

"That is true," said Father d'Aigrigny.

"It was then a desperate case, given up by the best doctors," continued Rodin, with irony, "and yet I have undertaken to restore it to life. Go on."

And, plunging both hands into the pockets of his trousers, he looked Father d'Aigrigny full in the face.

"Your reverence blamed me harshly," resumed Father d'Aigrigny, "not for having sought, by every possible means, to recover the property odiously diverted from our society—"

"All your casuists authorize you to do so," said the cardinal; "the texts are clear and positive; you have a right to recover; per fas aut nefas what has been treacherously taken from you."

"And therefore," resumed Father d'Aigrigny, "Father Rodin only reproached me with the military roughness of my means. 'Their violence,' he said, 'was in dangerous opposition to the manners of the age.' Be it so; but first of all, I could not be exposed to any legal proceedings, and, but for one fatal circumstance, success would have crowned the course I had taken, however rough and brutal it may appear. Now, may I ask your reverence what—"

"What I have done more than you?" said Rodin to Father d'Aigrigny, giving way to his impertinent habit of interrupting people; "what I have done better than you?—what step I have taken in the Rennepont affair, since I received it from you in a desperate condition? Is that what you wish to know?"

"Precisely," said Father d'Aigrigny, dryly.

"Well, I confess," resumed Rodin, in a sardonic tone, "just as you did great things, coarse things, turbulent things, I have been doing little, puerile, secret things. Oh, heaven! you cannot imagine what a foolish part I, who passed for a man of enlarged views, have been acting for the last six weeks."

"I should never have allowed myself to address such a reproach to your reverence, however deserved it may appear," said Father d'Aigrigny, with a bitter smile.

"A reproach?" said Rodin, shrugging his shoulders; "a reproach? You shall be the judge. Do you know what I wrote about you, some six weeks ago? Here it is: 'Father d'Aigrigny has excellent qualities. He will be of much service to me'—and from to-morrow I shall employ you very actively, added Rodin, by way of parenthesis—'but he is not great enough to know how to make himself little on occasion.' Do you understand?"

"Not very well," said Father d'Aigrigny, blushing.

"So much the worse for you," answered Rodin; "it only proves that I was right. Well, since I must tell you, I have been wise enough to play the most foolish part for six whole weeks. Yes, I have chatted nonsense with a grisette—have talked of liberty, progress, humanity, emancipation of women, with a young, excited girl; of Napoleon the Great, and all sorts of

Bonapartist idolatry, with an old, imbecile soldier; of imperial glory, humiliation of France, hopes in the King of Rome, with a certain marshal of France, who, with a heart full of adoration for the robber of thrones, that was transported to Saint-Helena, has a head as hollow and sonorous as a trumpet, into which you have only to blow some warlike or patriotic notes, and it will flourish away of itself, without knowing why or how. More than all this, I have talked of love affairs with a young tiger. When I told you it was lamentable to see a man of any intelligence descend, as I have done, to all such petty ways of connecting the thousand threads of this dark web, was I not right? Is it not a fine spectacle to see the spider obstinately weaving its net?—to see the ugly little black animal crossing thread upon thread, fastening it here, strengthening it there, and again lengthening it in some other place? You shrug your shoulders in pity; but return two hours after—what will you find? The little black animal eating its fill, and in its web a dozen of the foolish flies, bound so securely, that the little black animal has only to choose the moment of its repast."

As he uttered those words, Rodin smiled strangely; his eyes, gradually half closed, opened to their full width, and seemed to shine more than usual. The Jesuit felt a sort of feverish excitement, which he attributed to the contest in which he had engaged before these eminent personages, who already felt the influence of his original and cutting speech.

Father d'Aigrigny began to regret having entered on the contest. He resumed, however, with ill-repressed irony: "I do not dispute the smallness of your means. I agree with you, they are very puerile—they are even very vulgar. But that is not quite sufficient to give an exalted notion of your merit. May I be allowed to ask—"

"What these means have produced?" resumed Rodin, with an excitement that was not usual with him. "Look into my spider's web, and you will see there the beautiful and insolent young girl, so proud, six weeks ago, of her grace, mind, and audacity—now pale, trembling, mortally wounded at the heart."

"But the act of chivalrous intrepidity of the Indian prince, with which all Paris is ringing," said the princess, "must surely have touched Mdlle. de Cardoville."

"Yes; but I have paralyzed the effect of that stupid and savage devotion, by demonstrating to the young lady that it is not sufficient to kill black panthers to prove one's self a susceptible, delicate, and faithful lover."

"Be it so," said Father d'Aigrigny; "we will admit the fact that Mdlle. de Cardoville is wounded to the heart."

"But what does this prove with regard to the Rennepont affair?" asked the cardinal, with curiosity, as he leaned his elbows on the table.

"There results from it," said Rodin, "that when our most dangerous enemy is mortally wounded, she abandons the battlefield. That is something, I should imagine."

"Indeed," said the princess, "the talents and audacity of Mdlle. de Cardoville would make her the soul of the coalition formed against us."

"Be it so," replied Father d'Aigrigny, obstinately; "she may be no longer formidable in that respect. But the wound in her heart will not prevent her from inheriting."

"Who tells you so?" asked Rodin, coldly, and with assurance. "Do you know why I have taken such pains, first to bring her in contact with Djalma, and then to separate her from him?"

"That is what I ask you," said Father D'Aigrigny; "how can this storm of passion prevent Mdlle. de Cardoville and the prince from inheriting?"

"Is it from the serene, or from the stormy sky, that darts the destroying thunderbolt?" said Rodin, disdainfully. "Be satisfied; I shall know where to place the conductor. As for M. Hardy, the man lived for three things: his workmen, his friend, his mistress. He has been thrice wounded in the heart. I always take aim at the heart; it is legal and sure."

"It is legal, and sure, and praiseworthy," said the bishop; "for, if I understand you rightly, this manufacturer had a concubine; now it is well to make use of an evil passion for the punishment of the wicked."

"True, quite true," added the cardinal; "if they have evil passion for us to make use of it, it is their own fault."

"Our holy Mother Perpetue," said the princess, "took every means to discover this abominable adultery."

"Well, then, M. Hardy is wounded in his dearest affections, I admit," said Father d'Aigrigny, still disputing every inch of ground; "ruined too in his fortune, which will only make him the more eager after this inheritance."

The argument appeared of weight to the two prelates and the princess; all looked at Rodin with anxious curiosity. Instead of answering he walked up to the sideboard, and, contrary to his habits of stoical sobriety, and in spite of his repugnance for wine, he examined the decanters, and said: "What is there in them?"

"Claret and sherry," said the hostess, much astonished at the sudden taste of Rodin, "and—"

The latter took a decanter at hazard, and poured out a glass of Madeira, which he drank off at a draught. Just be fore he had felt a strange kind of shivering; to this had succeeded a sort of weakness. He hoped the wine would revive him.

After wiping his mouth with the back of his dirty hand, he returned to the table, and said to Father d'Aigrigny: "What did you tell me about M. Hardy?"

"That being ruined in fortune, he would be the more eager to obtain this immense inheritance," answered Father d'Aigrigny, inwardly much offended at the imperious tone.

"M. Hardy think of money?" said Rodin, shrugging his shoulders. "He is indifferent to life, plunged in a stupor from which he only starts to burst into tears. Then he speaks with mechanical kindness to those about him. I have placed him in good hands. He begins, however, to be sensible to the attentions shown him, for he is good, excellent, weak; and ii is to this excellence, Father d'Aigrigny, that you must appeal to finish the work in hand."

"I?" said Father d'Aigrigny, much surprised.

"Yes; and then you will find that the result I have obtained is considerable, and—"

Rodin paused, and, pressing his hand to his forehead, said to himself: "It is strange!"

"What is the matter?" said the princess, with interest.

"Nothing, madame," answered Rodin, with a shiver; "it is doubtless the wine I drank; I am not accustomed to it. I feel a slight headache; but it will pass."

"Your eyes are very bloodshot, my good father, said the princess.

"I have looked too closely into my web," answered the Jesuit, with a sinister smile; "and I must look again, to make Father d'Aigrigny, who pretends to be blind, catch a glimpse of my other flies. The two daughters of Marshal Simon, for instance, growing sadder and more dejected every day, at the icy barrier raised between them and their father; and the latter thinking himself one day dishonored if he does this, another if he does that; so that the hero of the Empire has become weaker and more irresolute than a child. What more remains of this impious family? Jacques Rennepont? Ask Morok, to what a state of debasement intemperance has reduced him, and towards what an abyss he is rushing!—There is my occurrence-sheet; you see to what are reduced all the members of this family, who, six weeks ago, had each elements of strength and union! Behold these Renneponts, who, by the will of their heretical ancestor, were to unite their forces to combat and crush our Society!—There was good reason to fear them; but what did I say? That I would act upon their passions. What have I done? I have acted upon their passions. At this hour they are vainly struggling in my web—they are mine—they are mine—"

As he was speaking, Rodin's countenance and voice had undergone a singular alteration; his complexion, generally so cadaverous, had become flushed, but unequally, and in patches; then, strange phenomenon! his eyes grew both more brilliant and more sunken, and his voice sharper and louder. The change in the countenance of Rodin, of which he did not appear to be conscious, was so remarkable, that the other actors in this scene looked at him with a sort of terror.

Deceived as to the cause of this impression, Rodin exclaimed with indignation, in a voice interrupted by deep gaspings for breath: "It is pity for this impious race, that I read upon your faces? Pity for the young girl, who never enters a church, and erects pagan altars in her habitation? Pity for Hardy, the sentimental blasphemer, the philanthropic atheist, who had no chapel in his factory, and dared to blend the names of Socrates, Marcus, Aurelius, and Plato, with our Savior's? Pity for the Indian worshipper of Brahma? Pity for the two sisters, who have never even been baptized? Pity for that brute, Jacques Rennepont? Pity for the stupid imperial soldier, who has Napoleon for his god, and the bulletins of the Grand Army for his gospel? Pity for this family of renegades, whose ancestor, a relapsed heretic, not content with robbing us of our property, excites from his tomb, at the end of a century and a half, his cursed race to lift their heads against us? What! to defend ourselves from these vipers, we shall not have the right to crush them in their own venom?—I tell you, that it is to serve heaven, and to give a salutary example to the world, to devote, by unchaining their own passions, this impious family to grief and despair and death!"

As he spoke thus, Rodin was dreadful in his ferocity; the fire of his eyes became still more brilliant; his lips were dry and burning, a cold sweat bathed his temples, which could be seen throbbing; an icy shudder ran through his frame. Attributing these symptoms to fatigue from writing through a portion of the night, and wishing to avoid fainting, he went to the sideboard, filled another glass with wine, which he drank off at a draught, and returned as the cardinal said to him: "If your course with regard to this family needed justification, my good father, your last word would have victoriously justified it. Not only are you right, according to your own casuists, but there is nothing in your proceedings contrary to human laws. As for the divine law, it is pleasing to the Lord to destroy impiety with its own weapons."

Conquered, as well as the others, by Rodin's diabolical assurance, and brought back to a kind of fearful admiration, Father d'Aigrigny said to him: "I confess I was wrong in doubting the judgment of your reverence. Deceived by the appearance of the means employed, I could not judge of their connection, and above all, of their results. I now see, that, thanks to you, success is no longer doubtful."

"This is an exaggeration," replied Rodin, with feverish impatience; "all these passions are at work, but the moment is critical. As the alchemist bends over the crucible, which may give him either treasures or sudden death—I alone at this moment—"

Rodin did not finish the sentence. He pressed both his hands to his forehead, with a stifled cry of pain.

"What is the matter?" said Father d'Aigrigny. "For some moments you have been growing fearfully pale."

"I do not know 'what is the matter," said Rodin, in an altered voice; "my headache increases—I am seized with a sort of giddiness."

"Sit down," said the princess, with interest.

"Take something," said the bishop.

"It will be nothing," said Rodin, with an effort; "I am no milksop, thank heaven!—I had little sleep last night; it is fatigue—nothing more. I was saying, that I alone could now direct this affair: but I cannot execute the plan myself. I must keep out of the way, and watch in the shade: I must hold the threads, which I alone can manage," added Rodin, in a faint voice.

"My good father," said the cardinal uneasily, "I assure you that you are very unwell. Your paleness is becoming livid."

"It is possible," answered Rodin, courageously; "but I am not to be so soon conquered. To return to our affair—this is the time, in which your qualities, Father d'Aigrigny, will turn to good account. I have never denied them, and they may now be of the greatest use. You have the power of charming—grace—eloquence—you must—"

Rodin paused again. A cold sweat poured from his forehead. He felt his legs give way under him, notwithstanding his obstinate energy.

"I confess, I am not well," he said; "yet, this morning, I was as well as ever. I shiver. I am icy cold."

"Draw near the fire—it is a sudden indisposition," said the bishop, offering his arm with heroic devotion; "it will not be anything of consequence."

"If you were to take something warm, a cup of tea," said the princess; "Dr. Baleinier will be here directly—he will reassure us as to this—indisposition."

"It is really inexplicable," said the prelate.

At these words of the cardinal, Rodin, who had advanced with difficulty towards the fire, turned his eyes upon the prelate, and looked at him fixedly in a strange manner, for about a second; then, strong in his unconquerable energy, notwithstanding the change in his features, which were now visibly disfigured, Rodin said, in a broken voice, which he tried to make firm: "The fire has warmed me; it will be nothing. I have no time to coddle myself. It would be a pretty thing to fall ill just as the Rennepont affair can only succeed by my exertions! Let us return to business. I told you, Father d'Aigrigny, that you might serve us a good deal; and you also, princess, who have espoused this cause as if it were your own—"

Rodin again paused. This time he uttered a piercing cry, sank upon a chair placed near him, and throwing himself back convulsively, he pressed his hands to his chest, and exclaimed: "Oh! what pain!"

Then (dreadful sight!) a cadaverous decomposition, rapid as thought, took place in Rodin's features. His hollow eyes were filled with blood, and seemed to shrink back in their orbits, which formed, as it were, two dark holes, in the centre of which blazed points of fire; nervous convulsions drew the flabby, damp, and icy skin tight over the bony prominences of the face, which was becoming rapidly green. From the lips, writhing with pain, issued the struggling breath, mingled with the words: "Oh! I suffer! I burn!"

Then, yielding to a transport of fury. Rodin tore with his nails his naked chest, for he had twisted off the buttons of his waistcoat, and rent his black and filthy shirt-front, as if the pressure of those garments augmented the violence of the pain under which he was writhing. The bishop, the cardinal, and Father d'Aigrigny, hastily approached Rodin, to try and hold him; he was seized with horrible convulsions; but, suddenly, collecting all his strength, he rose upon his feet stiff as a corpse. Then, with his garments in disorder, his thin, gray hair standing up all around his greenish face, fixing his red and flaming eyes upon the cardinal, he seized him with convulsive grasp, and exclaimed in a terrible voice, half stifled in his throat: "Cardinal Malipieri—this illness is too sudden—they suspect me at Rome—you are of the race of the Borgias—and your secretary was with me this morning!"

"Unhappy man! what does he dare insinuate?" cried the prelate, as amazed as he was indignant at the accusation. So saying, the cardinal strove to free himself from the grasp of Rodin, whose fingers were now as stiff as iron.

"I am poisoned!" muttered Rodin, and sinking back, he fell into the arms of Father d'Aigrigny.

Notwithstanding his alarm, the cardinal had time to whisper to the latter: "He thinks himself poisoned. He must therefore be plotting something very dangerous."

The door of the room opened. It was Dr. Baleinier.

"Oh, doctor!" cried the princess, as she ran pale and frightened towards him; "Father Rodin has been suddenly attacked with terrible convulsions. Quick! quick!"

"Convulsions? oh! it will be nothing, madame," said the doctor, throwing down his hat upon a chair, and hastily approaching the group which surrounded the sick man.

"Here is the doctor!" cried the princess. All stepped aside, except Father d'Aigrigny, who continued to support Rodin, leaning against a chair.

"Heavens! what symptoms!" cried Dr. Baleinier, examining with growing terror the countenance of Rodin, which from green was turning blue.

"What is it?" asked all the spectators, with one voice.

"What is it?" repeated the doctor, drawing back as if he had trodden upon a serpent. "It is the cholera! and contagious!"

On this frightful, magic word, Father d'Aigrigny abandoned his hold of Rodin, who rolled upon the floor.

"He is lost!" cried Dr. Baleinier. "But I will run to fetch the means for a last effort." And he rushed towards the door.

The Princess de Saint-Dizier, Father d'Aigrigny, the bishop, and the cardinal followed in terror the flight of Dr. Baleinier. They all pressed to the door, which, in their consternation, they could not open. It opened at last but from without—and Gabriel appeared upon the threshold. Gabriel, the type of the true priest, the holy, the evangelical minister, to whom we can never pay enough of respect and ardent sympathy, and tender admiration. His angelic countenance, in its mild serenity, offered a striking contrast of these faces, all disturbed and contracted with terror.

The young priest was nearly thrown down by the fugitives, who rushed through the now open doorway, exclaiming: "Do not go in! he is dying of the cholera. Fly!"

On these words, pushing back the bishop, who, being the last, was trying to force a passage, Gabriel ran towards Rodin, while the prelate succeeded in making his escape. Rodin, stretched upon the carpet, his limbs twisted with fearful cramps, was writhing in the extremity of pain. The violence of his fall had, no doubt, roused him to consciousness, for he moaned, in a sepulchral voice: "They leave me to die—like a dog—the cowards!—Help!—no one—"

And the dying man, rolling on his back with a convulsive movement, turned towards the ceiling a face on which was branded the infernal despair of the damned, as he once more repeated: "No one!—not one!"

His eyes, which suddenly flamed with fury, just then met the large blue eyes of the angelic and mild countenance of Gabriel who, kneeling beside him, said to him, in his soft, grave tones: "I am here, father—to help you, if help be possible—to pray for you, if God calls you to him."

"Gabriel!" murmured Rodin, with failing voice; "forgive me for the evil I have done you—do not leave me—do not—"

Rodin could not finish; he had succeeded in raising himself into a sitting posture; he now uttered a loud cry, and fell back without sense or motion.

The same day it was announced in the evening papers: "The cholera has broken out in Paris. The first case declared itself this day, at half past three, P.M. in the Rue de Babylone, at Saint-Dizier House."

CHAPTER XVIII.

THE SQUARE OF NOTRE DAME.

A week had passed since Rodin was seized with the cholera, and its ravages had continually increased. That was an awful time! A funeral pall was spread over Paris, once so gay. And yet, never had the sky been of a more settled, purer blue; never had the sun shone more brilliantly. The inexorable serenity of nature, during the ravages of the deadly scourge, offered a strange and mysterious contrast. The flaunting light of the dazzling sunshine fell full upon the features, contracted by a thousand agonizing fears. Each trembled for himself, or for those dear to him; every countenance was stamped with an expression of feverish astonishment and dread. People walked with rapid steps, as if they would escape from the fate which threatened them; besides, they were in haste to return to their homes, for often they left life, health, happiness, and, two hours later, they found agony, death, and despair.

At every moment, new dismal objects met the view. Sometimes carts passed along, filled with coffins, symmetrically piled; they stopped before every house. Men in black and gray garments were in waiting before the door; they held out their hands, and to some, one coffin was thrown, to some two, frequently three or four, from the same house. It sometimes happened that the store was quickly exhausted, and the cart, which had arrived full, went away empty, whilst many of the dead in the street were still unserved. In nearly every dwelling, upstairs and down, from the roof to the cellar, there was a stunning tapping of hammers: coffins were being nailed down, and so many, so very many were nailed, that sometimes those who worked stopped from sheer fatigue. Then broke forth laments, heart-rending moans, despairing imprecations. They were uttered by those from whom the men in black and gray had taken some one to fill the coffins.

Unceasingly were the coffins filled, and day and night did those men work, but by day more than by night, for, as soon as it was dusk, came a gloomy file of vehicles of all kinds—the usual hearses were not sufficient; but cars, carts, drays, hackney-coaches, and such like, swelled the funeral procession; different to the other conveyances, which entered the streets full and went away empty—these came empty but soon returned full. During that period, the windows of many houses were illuminated, and often the lights remained burning till the morning. It was "the season." These illuminations resembled the gleaming rays which shine in the gay haunts of pleasure; but there were tapers instead of wax candles, and the chanting of prayers for the dead replaced the murmur of the ball-room. In the streets, instead of the facetious transparencies which indicate the costumers, there swung at intervals huge lanterns of a blood-red color, with these words in black letters: "Assistance for those attacked with the cholera." The true places for revelry, during the night, were the churchyards; they ran riot—they, usually so desolate and silent, during the dark, quiet hours, when the cypress trees rustle in the breeze, so lonely, that no human step dared to disturb the solemn silence which reigned there at night, became on a sudden, animated, noisy, riotous, and resplendent with light. By the smoky flames of torches, which threw a red glare upon the dark fir-trees, and the white tombstones, many grave-diggers worked merrily, humming snatches of some favorite tune. Their laborious and hazardous industry then commanded a very high price; they were in such request that it was necessary to humor them. They drank often and much; they sang long and loud; and this to keep up their strength and spirits good, absolute requisites in such an employment. If, by chance, any did not finish the grave they had begun, some obliging comrade finished it for them (fitting expression!), and placed them in it with friendly care.

Other distant sounds responded to the joyous strains of the grave diggers; public-houses had sprung up in the neighborhood of the churchyards, and the drivers of the dead, when they had "set down their customers," as they jocosely expressed themselves, enriched with their unusual gratuities, feasted and made merry like lords; dawn often found them with a glass in their hands, and a jest on their lips; and, strange to say, among these funeral satellites, who breathed the very atmosphere of the disease, the mortality was scarcely perceptible. In the dark, squalid quarters of the town, where, surrounded by infectious exhalations, the indigent population was crowded together, and miserable beings, exhausted by severe privation, were "bespoke" by the cholera, as it was energetically said at the time, not only individuals, but whole families, were carried off in a few hours; and yet, sometimes, oh, merciful Providence! one or two little children were left in the cold and empty room, after the father and mother, brother and sister, had been taken away in their shells.

Frequently, houses which had swarmed with hard working laborers, were obliged to be shut up for want of tenants; in one day, they had been completely cleared by this terrible visitation, from the cellars, where little chimney-sweepers slept upon straw, to the garret, on whose cold brick floor lay stretched some wan and half-naked being, without work and without bread. But, of all the wards of Paris, that which perhaps presented the most frightful spectacle during the progress of the cholera, was the City; and in the City, the square before the cathedral of Notre-Dame was almost every day the theatre of dreadful scenes: for this locality was frequently thronged with those who conveyed the sick from the neighboring streets to the Great Hospital. The cholera had not one aspect, but a thousand. So that one week after Rodin had been suddenly attacked, several events combining the horrible and the grotesque occurred in the square of Notre Dame.

Instead of the Rue d'Arcole, which now leads directly to the square, it was then approached on one side, by a mean, narrow lane, like all the other streets of the City, and terminating in a dark, low archway. Upon entering the square the principal door of the huge Cathedral was to the left of the spectator, and facing him were the Hospital buildings. A little beyond, was an opening which gave to view a portion of the parapet of the Quay Notre-Dame. A placard had been recently stuck on the discolored and sunken wall of the archway; it contained these words, traced in large characters.[37]

"VENGEANCE! VENGEANCE!

"The Working-men carried to the hospitals are poisoned, because the number of patients is too great; every night, Boats filled with corpses, drop down the Seine.

"Vengeance and Death to the murderers of the People!"

Two men, enveloped in cloaks, and half-hidden in the deep shadow of the vault, were listening with anxious curiosity to the threatening murmur, which rose with increasing force from among a tumultuous assembly, grouped around the Hospital. Soon, cries of "Death to the doctors!—Vengeance!" reached the ears of the persons who were in ambush under the arch.

"The posters are working," said one; "the train is on fire. When once the populace is roused, we can set them on whom we please."

"I say," replied the other man, "look over there. That Hercules, whose athletic form towers above the mob, was cue of the most frantic leaders when M. Hardy's factory was destroyed."

"To be sure he was; I know him again. Wherever mischief is to be done, you are sure to find those vagabonds.

"Now, take my advice, do not let us remain under this archway," said the other man; "the wind is as cold as ice, and though I am cased in flannel—"

"You are right, the cholera is confoundedly impolite. Besides, everything is going on well here; I am likewise assured that the whole of the Faubourg Saint-Antoine is ready to rise in the republican cause; that will serve our ends, and our holy religion will triumph over revolutionary impiety. Let us rejoin Father d'Aigrigny."

"Where shall we find him?"

"Near here, come—come."

The two hastily disappeared.

The sun, beginning to decline, shed its golden rays upon the blackened sculptures of the porch of Notre-Dame, and upon its two massy towers, rising in imposing majesty against a perfectly blue sky, for during the fast few days, a north-east wind, dry and cold, had driven away the lightest cloud. A considerable number of people, as we have already stated, obstructed the approach to the Hospital; they crowded round the iron railings that protect the front of the building, behind which was stationed a detachment of infantry, the cries of "Death to the doctors!" becoming every moment more threatening. The people who thus vociferated. belonged to an idle, vagabond, and depraved populace—the dregs of the Paris mob; and (terrible spectacle!) the unfortunate beings who were forcibly carried through the midst of these hideous groups entered the Hospital, whilst the air resounded with hoarse clamors, and cries of "Death." Every moment, fresh victims were brought along in litters, and on stretchers; the litters were frequently furnished with coarse curtains, and thus the sick occupants were concealed from the public gaze; but the stretchers, having no covering, the convulsive movements of the dying patients often thrust aside the sheet, and exposed to view their faces, livid as corpses. Far from inspiring with terror the wretches assembled round the Hospital, such spectacles became to them the signal for savage jests, and atrocious predictions upon the fate of these poor creatures, when once in the power of the doctors.

The big blaster and Ciboule, with a good many of their adherents, were among the mob. After the destruction of Hardy's factory, the quarryman was formally expelled from the union of the Wolves, who would have nothing more to do with this wretch; since then, he had plunged into the grossest debauchery, and speculating on his herculean strength, had hired himself as the officious champion of Ciboule and her compeers. With the exception therefore of some chance passengers, the square of Notre-Dame was filled with a ragged crowd, composed of the refuse of the Parisian populace—wretches who call for pity as well as blame; for misery, ignorance, and destitution, beget but too fatally vice and crime. These savages of civilization felt neither pity, improvement, nor terror, at the shocking sights with which they were surrounded; careless of a life which was a daily struggle against hunger, or the allurements of guilt, they braved the pestilence with infernal audacity, or sank under it with blasphemy on their lips.

The tall form of the quarryman was conspicuous amongst the rest; with inflamed eyes and swollen features, he yelled at the top of his voice: "Death to the body-snatchers! they poison the people."

"That is easier than to feed them," added Ciboule. Then, addressing herself to an old man, who was being carried with great difficulty through the dense crowd, upon a chair, by two men, the hag continued: "Hey? don't go in there, old croaker; die here in the open air instead of dying in that den, where you'll be doctored like an old rat."

"Yes," added the quarryman; "and then they'll throw you into the water to feast the fishes, which you won't swallow any more."

At these atrocious cries, the old man looked wildly around, and uttered faint groans. Ciboule wished to stop the persons who were carrying him, and they had much difficulty in getting rid of the hag. The number of cholera-patients arriving increased every moment, and soon neither litters nor stretchers could be obtained, so that they were borne along in the arms of the attendants. Several awful episodes bore witness to the startling rapidity of the infection. Two men were carrying a stretcher covered with a blood-stained sheet; one of them suddenly felt himself attacked with the complaint; he stopped short, his powerless arms let go the stretcher; he turned pale, staggered, fell upon the patient, becoming as livid as him; the other man, struck with terror, fled precipitately, leaving his companion and the dying man in the midst of the crowd. Some drew back in horror, others burst into a savage laugh.

"The horses have taken fright," said the quarryman, "and have left the turn-out in the lurch."

"Help!" cried the dying man, with a despairing accent; "for pity's sake take me in."

"There's no more room in the pit," said one, in a jeering tone.

"And you've no legs left to reach the gallery," added another.

The sick man made an effort to rise; but his strength failed him; he fell back exhausted on the mattress. A sudden movement took place among the crowd, the stretcher was overturned, the old man and his companion were trodden underfoot, and their groans were drowned in the cries of "Death to the body-snatchers!" The yells were renewed with fresh fury, but the ferocious band, who respected nothing in their savage fury, were soon after obliged to open their ranks to several workmen, who vigorously cleared the way for two of their friends carrying in their arms a poor artisan. He was still young, but his heavy and already livid head hung down upon the shoulder of one of them. A little child followed, sobbing, and holding by one of the workmen's coats. The measured and sonorous sound of several drums was now heard at a distance in the winding streets of the city: they were beating the call to arms, for sedition was rife in the Faubourg Saint-Antoine. The drummers emerged from under the archway, and were traversing the square, when one of them, a gray-haired veteran, suddenly slackened the rolling of his drum, and stood still: his companions turned round in surprise—he had turned green; his legs gave way, he stammered some unintelligible words, and had fallen upon the pavement before those in the front rank had time to pause. The overwhelming rapidity of this attack startled for a moment the most hardened among the surrounding spectators; for, wondering at the interruption, a part of the crowd had rushed towards the soldiers.

At sight of the dying man, supported in the arms of two of his comrades, one of the individuals, who, concealed under the arch, had watched the beginning of the popular excitement, said to the drummers: "Your comrade drank, perhaps, at some fountain on the road?"

"Yes, sir," replied one; "he was very thirsty; he drank two mouthfuls of water on the Place du Chatelet."

"Then he is poisoned," said the man.

"Poisoned?" cried several voices.

"It is not surprising," replied the man, in a mysterious tone; "poison is thrown into the public fountains; and this very morning a man was massacred in the Rue Beaubourg who was discovered emptying a paper of arsenic into a pot of wine at a public-house."[38]

Having said these words, the man disappeared in the crowd. This report, no less absurd than the tales about the poisoning of the Hospital patients, was received with a general burst of indignation. Five or six ragged beings, regular ruffians, seized the body of the expiring drummer, hoisted it upon their shoulders, in spite of all the efforts of his comrades to prevent them, and paraded the square exhibiting the dismal trophy. Ciboule and the quarryman went before, crying: "Wake way for the corpse! This is how they poison the people!"

A fresh incident now attracted the attention of the crowd. A travelling carriage, which had not been able to pass along the Quai-Napoleon, the pavement of which was up, had ventured among the intricate streets of the city, and now arrived in the square of Notre-Dame on its way to the other side of the Seine. Like many others, its owners were flying from Paris, to escape the pestilence which decimated it. A man-servant and a lady's maid were in the rumble, and they exchanged a glance of alarm as they passed the Hospital, whilst a young man seated in the front part of the carriage let down the glass, and called to the postilions to go slowly, for fear of accident, as the crowd was very dense at that part of the square. This young man was Lord Morinval, and on the back seat were Lord Montbron and his niece, Lady Morinval. The pale and anxious countenance of the young lady showed the alarm which she felt; and Montbron, notwithstanding his firmness of mind, appeared to be very uneasy; he, as well as his niece, frequently had recourse to a smelling-bottle filled with camphor.

During the last few minutes, the carriage had advanced very slowly, the postilions managing their horses with great caution, when a sudden hubbub, at first distant and undefined, but soon more distinct, arose among the throng, as it drew near, the ringing sound of chains and metal, peculiar to the artillery-wagons, was plainly audible, and presently one of these vehicles came towards the travelling-carriage, from the direction of the Quai Notre-Dame. It seemed strange, that though the crowd was so compact, yet at the rapid approach of this wagon, the close ranks of human beings opened as if by enchantment, but the following words which were passed from mouth to mouth soon accounted for the prodigy: "A wagon full of dead! the wagon of the dead!" As we have already stated, the usual funeral conveyances were no longer sufficient for the removal of the corpses; a number of artillery wagons had been put into requisition, and the coffins were hastily piled in these novel hearses.

Many of the spectators regarded this gloomy vehicle with dismay, but the quarryman and his band redoubled their horrible jokes.

"Make way for the omnibus of the departed!" cried Ciboule.

"No danger of having one's toes crushed in that omnibus," said the quarryman.

"Doubtless they're easy to please, the stiff-uns in there."

"They never want to be set down, at all events."

"I say, there's only one reg'lar on duty as postilion!"

"That's true, the leaders are driven by a man in a smock-frock."

"Oh! I daresay the other soldier was tired, lazy fellow! and got into the omnibus with the others—they'll all get out at the same big hole."

"Head foremost, you know."

"Yes, they pitch them head first into a bed of lime."

"Why, one might follow the dead-cart blind-fold, and no mistake. It's worse than Montfaucon knacker-yards!"

"Ha! ha! ha!—it's rather gamey!" said the quarryman, alluding to the infectious and cadaverous odor which this funeral conveyance left behind it.

"Here's sport!" exclaimed Ciboule: "the omnibus of the dead will run against the fine coach. Hurrah! the rich folks will smell death."

Indeed, the wagon was now directly in front of the carriage, and at a very little distance from it. A man in a smock-frock and wooden shoes drove the two leaders, and an artilleryman the other horses. The coffins were so piled up within this wagon, that its semicircular top did not shut down closely, so that, as it jolted heavily over the uneven pavement, the biers could be seen chafing against each other. The fiery eyes and inflamed countenance of the man in the smock-frock showed that he was half intoxicated; urging on the horses with his voice, his heels, and his whip, he paid no attention to the remonstrances of the soldier, who had great difficulty in restraining his own animals, and was obliged to follow the irregular movements of the carman. Advancing in this disorderly manner, the wagon deviated from its course just as it should have passed the travelling-carriage, and ran against it. The shock forced open the top, one of the coffins was thrown out, and, after damaging the panels of the carriage, fell upon the pavement with a dull and heavy sound. The deal planks had been hastily nailed together, and were shivered in the fall, and from the wreck of the coffin rolled a livid corpse, half enveloped in a shroud.

At this horrible spectacle, Lady Morinval, who had mechanically leaned forward, gave a loud scream, and fainted. The crowd fell back in dismay; the postilions, no less alarmed, took advantage of the space left open to them by the retreat of the multitude; they whipped their horses, and the carriage dashed on towards the quay. As it disappeared behind the furthermost buildings of the Hospital, the shrill joyous notes of distant trumpets were heard, and repeated shouts proclaimed: "The Cholera Masquerade!" The words announced one of those episodes combining buffoonery with terror, which marked the period when the pestilence was on the increase, though now they can with difficulty be credited. If the evidence of eyewitnesses did not agree in every particular with the accounts given in the public papers of this masquerade, they might be regarded as the ravings of some diseased brain, and not as the notice of a fact which really occurred.

"The Masquerade of the Cholera" appeared, we say, in the square of Notre Dame, just as Morinval's carriage gained the quay, after disengaging itself from the death-wagon.

[37] It is well-known that at the time of the cholera, such placards were numerous in Paris, and were alternately attributed to opposite parties.

Among others, to the priests, many of the bishops having published mandatory letters, or stated openly in the churches of their diocese, that the Almighty had sent the cholera as a punishment to France for having driven away its lawful sovereign, and assimilated the Catholic to other forms of worship.

[38] It is notorious, that at this unhappy period several persons were massacred, under a false accusation of poisoning the fountains, etc.

CHAPTER XIX.

THE CHOLERA MASQUERADE.[39]

A stream of people, who preceded the masquerade, made a sudden irruption through the arch into the square, uttering loud cheers as they advanced. Children were also there, blowing horns, whilst some hooted and others hissed.

The quarryman, Ciboule, and their band, attracted by this new spectacle, rushed tumultuously towards the arch. Instead of the two eating-houses, which now (1845) stand on either side of the Rue d'Arcole, there was then only one, situated to the left of the vaulted passage, and much celebrated amongst the joyous community of students, for the excellence both of its cookery and its wines. At the first blare of the trumpets, sounded by the outriders in livery who preceded the masquerade, the windows of the great room of the eating-house were thrown open, and several waiters, with their napkins under their arms, leaned forward, impatient to witness the arrival of the singular guests they were expecting.

At length, the grotesque procession made its appearance in the thick of an immense uproar. The train comprised a chariot, escorted by men and women on horseback, clad in rich and elegant fancy dresses. Most of these maskers belonged to the middle and easy classes of society. The report had spread that masquerade was in preparation, for the purpose of daring the cholera, and, by this joyous demonstration, to revive the courage of the affrighted populace. Immediately, artists, young men about town, students, and so on, responded to the appeal, and though till now unknown one to the other, they easily fraternized together. Many brought their mistresses, to complete the show. A subscription had been opened to defray the expenses, and, that morning, after a splendid breakfast at the other end of Paris, the joyous troop had started bravely on their march, to finish the day by a dinner in the square of Notre Dame.

We say bravely, for it required a singular turn of mind, a rare firmness of character, in young women, to traverse, in this fashion, a great city plunged in consternation and terror—to fall in at every step with litters loaded with the dying, and carriages filled with the dead—to defy, as it were, in a spirit of strange pleasantry, the plague that was detonating the Parisians. It is certain that, in Paris alone, and there only amongst a peculiar class, could such an idea have ever been conceived or realized. Two men, grotesquely disguised as postilions at a funeral, with formidable false noses, rose-colored crape hat-bands and large favors of roses and crape bows at their buttonholes, rode before the vehicle. Upon the platform of the car were groups of allegorical personages, representing WINE, PLEASURE, LOVE, PLAY. The mission of these symbolical beings was, by means of jokes, sarcasms, and mockeries, to plague the life out of Goodman Cholera, a sort of funeral and burlesque Cassander, whom they ridiculed and made game of in a hundred ways. The moral of the play was this: "To brave Cholera in security, let us drink, laugh, game, and make love!"

WINE was represented by a huge, lusty Silenus, thick-set, and with swollen paunch, a crown of ivy on his brow, a panther's skin across his shoulder, and in his hand a large gilt goblet, wreathed with flowers. None other than Ninny Moulin, the famous moral and religious writer, could have exhibited to the astonished and delighted spectators an ear of so deep a scarlet, so majestic an abdomen, and a face of such triumphant and majestic fulness. Every moment, Ninny Moulin appeared to empty his cup—after which he burst out laughing in the face of Goodman Cholera. Goodman Cholera, a cadaverous pantaloon, was half-enveloped in a shroud; his mask of greenish cardboard, with red, hollow eyes, seemed every moment to grin as in mockery of death; from beneath his powdered peruke, surmounted by a pyramidical cotton night-cap, appeared his neck and arm, dyed of a bright green color; his lean hand, which shook almost always with a feverish trembling (not feigned, but natural), rested upon a crutch-handled cane; finally, as was becoming in a pantaloon, he wore red stockings, with buckles at the knees, and high slippers of black beaver. This grotesque representative of the cholera was Sleepinbuff.

Notwithstanding a slow and dangerous fever, caused by the excessive use of brandy, and by constant debauchery, that was silently undermining his constitution, Jacques Rennepont had been induced by Morok to join the masquerade. The brute-tamer himself, dressed as the King of Diamonds, represented PLAY. His forehead was adorned with a diadem of gilded paper, his face was pale and impassible, and as his long, yellow beard fell down the front of his parti-colored robe, Morok looked exactly the character he personated. From time to time, with an air of grave mockery, he shook close to the eyes of Goodman Cholera a large bag full of sounding counters, and on this bag were painted all sorts of playing cards. A certain stiffness in the right arm showed that the lion-tamer had not yet quite recovered from the effects of the wound which the panther had inflicted before being stabbed by Djalma.

PLEASURE, who also represented Laughter, classically shook her rattle, with its sonorous gilded bells, close to the ears of Goodman Cholera. She was a quick, lively young girl, and her fine black hair was crowned with a scarlet cap of liberty. For Sleepinbuff's sake, she had taken the place of the poor Bacchanal queen, who would not have failed to attend on such an occasion—she, who had been so valiant and gay, when she bore her part in a less philosophical, but not less amusing masquerade. Another pretty creature, Modeste Bornichoux, who served as a model to a painter of renown (one of the cavaliers of the procession), was eminently successful in her representation of LOVE. He could not have had a more charming face, and more graceful form. Clad in a light blue spangled tunic, with a blue and silver band across her chestnut hair, and little transparent wings affixed to her white shoulders, she placed one forefinger upon the other, and pointed with the prettiest impertinence at Goodman Cholera. Around the principal group, other maskers, more or less grotesque in appearance, waved each a banner, an which were inscriptions of a very anacreontic character, considering the circumstances:

"Down with the Cholera!" "Short and sweet!" "Laugh away, laugh always!" "We'll collar the Cholera!" "Love forever!" "Wine forever!" "Come if you dare, old terror!"

There was really such audacious gayety in this masquerade, that the greater number of the spectators, at the moment when it crossed the square, in the direction of the eating-house, where dinner was waiting, applauded it loudly and repeatedly. This sort of admiration, which courage, however mad and blind, almost always inspires, appeared to others (a small number, it must be confessed) a kind of defiance to the wrath of heaven; and these received the procession with angry murmurs. This extraordinary spectacle, and the different impressions it produced, were too remote from all customary facts to admit of a just appreciation. We hardly know if this daring bravado was deserving of praise or blame.

Besides, the appearance of those plagues, which from age to age decimate the population of whole countries, has almost always been accompanied by a sort of mental excitement, which none of those who have been spared by the contagion can hope to escape. It is a strange fever of the mind, which sometimes rouses the most stupid prejudices and the most ferocious passions, and sometimes inspires, on the contrary, the most magnificent devotion, the most courageous actions—with some, driving the fear of death to a point of the wildest terror—with others, exciting the contempt of life to express itself in the most audacious bravadoes. Caring little for the praise or blame it might deserve, the masquerade arrived before the eating-house, and made its entry in the midst of universal acclamations. Everything seemed to combine to give full effect to this strange scene, by the opposition of the most singular contrasts. Thus the tavern, in which was to be held this extraordinary feast, being situated at no great distance from the antique cathedral, and the gloomy hospital, the religious anthems of the ancient temple, the cries of the dying, and the bacchanalian songs of the banqueteers, must needs mingle, and by turns drown one another. The maskers now got down from their chariot, and from their horses, and went to take their places at the repast, which was waiting for them. The actors in the masquerade are at table in the great room of the tavern. They are joyous, noisy, even riotous. Yet their gayety has a strange tone, peculiar to itself.

Sometimes, the most resolute involuntarily remember that their life is at stake in this mad and audacious game with destiny. That fatal thought is rapid as the icy fever-shudder, which chills you in an instant; therefore, from time to time, an abrupt silence, lasting indeed only for a second, betrays these passing emotions which are almost immediately effaced by new bursts of joyful acclamation, for each one says to himself: "No weakness! my chum and my girl are looking at me!"

And all laugh, and knock glasses together, and challenge the next man, and drink out of the glass of the nearest woman. Jacques had taken off the mask and peruke of Goodman Cholera. His thin, leaden features, his deadly paleness, the lurid brilliancy of his hollow eyes, showed the incessant progress of the slow malady which was consuming this unfortunate man, brought by excesses to the last extremity of weakness. Though he felt the slow fire devouring his entrails, he concealed his pain beneath a forced and nervous smile.

To the left of Jacques was Morok, whose fatal influence was ever on the increase, and to his right the girl disguised as PLEASURE. She was named Mariette. By her side sat Ninny Moulin, in all his majestic bulk, who often pretended to be looking for his napkin under the table, in order to have the opportunity of pressing the knees of his other neighbor, Modeste, the representative of LOVE. Most of the guests were grouped according to their several tastes, each tender pair together, and the bachelors where they could. They had reached the second course, and the excellence of the wine, the good cheer, the gay speeches, and even the singularity of the occasion, had raised their spirits to a high degree of excitement, as may be gathered from the extraordinary incidents of the following scene.

[39] We read in the Constitutionnel, Saturday March 31st, 1832: "The Parisians readily conform to that part of the official instructions with regard to the cholera, which prescribes, as a preservation from the disease, not to be afraid, to amuse one's self, etc. The pleasures of Mid-Lent have been as brilliant and as mad as those of the carnival itself. For a long time past there had not been so many balls at this period of the year. Even the cholera has been made the subject of an itinerant caricature."

CHAPTER XX.

THE DEFIANCE.

Two or three times, without being remarked by the guests, one of the waiters had come to whisper to his fellows, and point with expressive gesture to the ceiling. But his comrades had taken small account of his observations or fears, not wishing, doubtless, to disturb the guests, whose mad gayety seemed ever on the increase.

"Who can doubt now of the superiority of our manner of treating this impertinent Cholera? Has he dared even to touch our sacred battalion?" said a magnificent mountebank-Turk, one of the standard-bearers of the masquerade.

"Here is all the mystery," answered another. "It is very simple. Only laugh in the face of the plague, and it will run away from you."

"And right enough too, for very stupid work it does," added a pretty little Columbine, emptying her glass.

"You are right, my darling; it is intolerably stupid work," answered the Clown belonging to the Columbine; "here you are very quiet, enjoying life, and all on a sudden you die with an atrocious grimace. Well! what then? Clever, isn't it? I ask you, what does it prove?"

"It proves," replied an illustrious painter of the romantic school, disguised like a Roman out of one of David's pictures, "it proves that the Cholera is a wretched colorist, for he has nothing but a dirty green on his pallet. Evidently he is a pupil of Jacobus, that king of classical painters, who are another species of plagues."

"And yet, master," added respectfully a pupil of the great painter, "I have seen some cholera patients whose convulsions were rather fine, and their dying looks first-rate!"

"Gentlemen," cried a sculptor of no less celebrity, "the question lies in a nutshell. The Cholera is a detestable colorist, but a good draughtsman. He shows you the skeleton in no time. By heaven! how he strips off the flesh!—Michael Angelo would be nothing to him."

"True," cried they all, with one voice; "the Cholera is a bad colorist, but a good draughtsman."

"Moreover, gentlemen," added Ninny Moulin, with comic gravity, "this plague brings with it a providential lesson, as the great Bossuet would have said."

"The lesson! the lesson!"

"Yes, gentlemen; I seem to hear a voice from above, proclaiming: 'Drink of the best, empty your purse, and kiss your neighbor's wife; for your hours are perhaps numbered, unhappy wretch!'"

So saying, the orthodox Silenus took advantage of a momentary absence of mind on the part of Modeste, his neighbor, to imprint on the blooming cheek of LOVE a long, loud kiss. The example was contagious, and a storm of kisses was mingled with bursts of laughter.

"Ha! blood and thunder!" cried the great painter as he gayly threatened Ninny Moulin; "you are very lucky that to-morrow will perhaps be the end of the world, or else I should pick a quarrel with you for having kissed my lovely LOVE."

"Which proves to you, O Rubens! O Raphael! the thousand advantages of the
Cholera, whom I declare to be essentially sociable and caressing."

"And philanthropic," said one of the guests; "thanks to him, creditors take care of the health of their debtors. This morning a usurer, who feels a particular interest in my existence, brought me all sorts of anti-choleraic drugs, and begged me to make use of them."

"And I!" said the pupil of the great painter. "My tailor wished to force me to wear a flannel band next to the skin, because I owe him a thousand crowns. But I answered 'Oh, tailor, give me a receipt in full, and I will wrap myself up in flannel, to preserve you my custom!'"

"O Cholera, I drink to thee!" said Ninny Moulin, by way of grotesque invocation. "You are not Despair; on the contrary, you are the emblem of Hope—yes, of hope. How many husbands, how many wives, longed for a number (alas! too uncertain chance) in the lottery of widowhood! You appear, and their hearts are gladdened. Thanks to you, benevolent pest! their chances of liberty are increased a hundredfold."

"And how grateful heirs ought to be! A cold—a heat—a trifle—and there, in an hour, some old uncle becomes a revered benefactor!"

"And those who are always looking out for other people's places—what an ally they must find in the Cholera!"

"And how true it will make many vows of constancy!" said Modeste, sentimentally. "How many villains have sworn to a poor, weak woman, to love her all their lives, who never meant (the wretches!) to keep their word so well!"

"Gentlemen," cried Ninny Moulin, "since we are now, perhaps, at the eve of the end of the world, as yonder celebrated painter has expressed it, I propose to play the world topsy-turvy: I beg these ladies to make advances to us, to tease us, to excite us, to steal kisses from us, to take all sorts of liberties with us, and (we shall not die of it) even to insult us. Yes, I declare that I will allow myself to be insulted. So, LOVE, you may offer me the greatest insult that can be offered to a virtuous and modest bachelor," added the religious writer, leaning over towards his neighbor, who repulsed him with peals of laughter; and the proposal of Ninny Moulin being received with general hilarity, a new impulse was given to the mirth and riot.

In the midst of the uproar, the waiter, who had before entered the room several times, to whisper uneasily to his comrades, whilst he pointed to the ceiling, again appeared with a pale and agitated countenance; approaching the man who performed the office of butler, he said to him, in a low voice, tremulous with emotion: "They are come!"

"Who?"

"You know—up there"; and he pointed to the ceiling.

"Oh!" said the butler, becoming thoughtful; "where are they?"

"They have just gone upstairs; they are there now," answered the waiter, shaking his head with an air of alarm; "yes, they are there!"

"What does master say?"

"He is very vexed, because—" and the waiter glanced round at the guests. "He does not know what to do; he has sent me to you."

"What the devil have I to do with it?" said the other; wiping his forehead. "It was to be expected, and cannot be helped."

"I will not remain here till they begin."

"You may as well go, for your long face already attracts attention. Tell master we must wait for the upshot."

The above incident was scarcely perceived in the midst of the growing tumult of the joyous feast. But, among the guests, one alone laughed not, drank not. This was Jacques. With fixed and lurid eye, he gazed upon vacancy. A stranger to what was passing around him, the unhappy man thought of the Bacchanal Queen, who had been so gay and brilliant in the midst of similar saturnalia. The remembrance of that one being, whom he still loved with an extravagant love, was the only thought that from time to time roused him from his besotted state.

It is strange, but Jacques had only consented to join this masquerade because the mad scene reminded him of the merry day he had spent with Cephyse—that famous breakfast, after a night of dancing, in which the Bacchanal Queen, from some extraordinary presentiment, had proposed a lugubrious toast with regard to this very pestilence, which was then reported to be approaching France. "To the Cholera!" had she said. "Let him spare those who wish to live, and kill at the same moment those who dread to part!"

And now, at this time, remembering those mournful words, Jacques was absorbed in painful thought. Morok perceived his absence of mind, and said aloud to him, "You have given over drinking, Jacques. Have you had enough wine? Then you will want brandy. I will send for some."

"I want neither wine nor brandy," answered Jacques, abruptly, and he fell back into a sombre reverie.

"Well, you may be right," resumed Morok, in a sardonic tone, and raising his voice still higher. "You do well to take care of yourself. I was wrong to name brandy in these times. There would be as much temerity in facing a bottle of brandy as the barrel of a loaded pistol."

On hearing his courage as a toper called in question, Sleepinbuff looked angrily at Morok. "You think it is from cowardice that I will not drink brandy!" cried the unfortunate man, whose half-extinguished intellect was roused to defend what he called his dignity. "Is it from cowardice that I refuse, d'ye think, Morok? Answer me!"

"Come, my good fellow, we have all shown our pluck today," said one of the guests to Jacques; "you, above all, who, being rather indisposed, yet had the courage to take the part of Goodman Cholera."

"Gentlemen," resumed Morok, seeing the general attention fixed upon himself and Sleepinbuff, "I was only joking; for if my comrade (pointing to Jacques) had the imprudence to accept my offer, it would be an act, not of courage, but of foolhardiness. Luckily, he has sense enough to renounce a piece of boasting so dangerous at this time, and I—"

"Waiter!" cried Jacques, interrupting Morok with angry impatience, "two bottles of brandy, and two glasses!"

"What are you going to do?" said Morok, with pretended uneasiness. "Why do you order two bottles of brandy?"

"For a duel," said Jacques, in a cool, resolute tone.

"A duel!" cried the spectators, in surprise.

"Yes," resumed Jacques, "a duel with brandy. You pretend there is as much danger in facing a bottle of brandy as a loaded pistol; let us each take a full bottle, and see who will be the first to cry quarter."

This strange proposition was received by some with shouts of joy, and by others with genuine uneasiness.

"Bravo! the champions of the bottle!" cried the first.

"No, no; there would be too much danger in such a contest," said the others.

"Just now," added one of the guests; "this challenge is as serious as an invitation to fight to the death."

"You hear," said Morok, with a diabolical smile, "you hear, Jacques? Will you now retreat before the danger?"

At these words, which reminded him of the peril to which he was about to expose himself, Jacques started, as if a sudden idea had occurred to him. He raised his head proudly, his cheeks were slightly flushed, his eye shone with a kind of gloomy satisfaction, and he exclaimed in a firm voice: "Hang it, waiter! are you deaf? I asked you for two bottles of brandy."

"Yes, sir," said the waiter, going to fetch them, although himself frightened at what might be the result of this bacchanalian struggle. But the mad and perilous resolution of Jacques was applauded by the majority.

Ninny Moulin moved about on his chair, stamped his feet, and shouted with all his might: "Bacchus and drink! bottles and glasses! the throats are dry! brandy to the rescue! Largess! largess!"

And, like a true champion of the tournament, he embraced Modeste, adding, to excuse the liberty: "Love, you shall be the Queen of Beauty, and I am only anticipating the victor's happiness!"

"Brandy to the rescue!" repeated they all, in chorus. "Largess!"

"Gentlemen," added Ninny Moulin, with enthusiasm, "shall we remain indifferent to the noble example set us by Goodman Cholera? He said in his pride, 'brandy!' Let us gloriously answer, 'punch!'"

"Yes, yes! punch!"

"Punch to the rescue!"

"Waiter!" shouted the religious writer, with the voice of a Stentor, "waiter! have you a pan, a caldron, a hogshead, or any other immensity, in which we can brew a monster punch?"

"A Babylonian punch!"

"A lake of punch!"

"An ocean of punch!"

Such was the ambitious crescendo that followed the proposition of Ninny Moulin.

"Sir," answered the waiter, with an air of triumph, "we just happen to have a large copper caldron, quite new. It has been used, and would hold at least thirty bottles."

"Bring the caldron!" said Ninny Moulin, majestically.

"The caldron forever!" shouted the chorus.

"Put in twenty bottles of brandy, six loaves of sugar, a dozen lemons, a pound of cinnamon, and then—fire! fire!" shouted the religious writer, with the most vociferous exclamations.

"Yes, yes! fire!" repeated the chorus!

The proposition of Ninny Moulin gave a new impetus to the general gayety; the most extravagant remarks were mingled with the sound of kisses, taken or given under the pretext that perhaps there would be no to-morrow, that one must make the most of the present, etc., etc. Suddenly, in one of the moments of silence which sometimes occur in the midst of the greatest tumult, a succession of slow and measured taps sounded above the ceiling of the banqueting-room. All remained silent, and listened.

CHAPTER XXI.

BRANDY TO THE RESCUE.

After the lapse of some seconds, the singular rapping which had so much surprised the guests, was again heard, but this time louder and longer.

"Waiter!" cried one of the party, "what in the devil's name is knocking?"

The waiter, exchanging with his comrades a look of uneasiness and alarm, stammered Out in reply: "Sir—it is—it is—"

"Well! I suppose it is some crabbed, cross-grained lodger, some animal, the enemy of joy, who is pounding on the floor of his room to warn us to sing less loud," said Ninny Moulin.

"Then, by a general rule," answered sententiously the pupil of the great painter, "if lodger or landlord ask for silence, tradition bids us reply by an infernal uproar, destined to drown all his remonstrances. Such, at least," added the scapegrace, modestly, "are the foreign relations that I have always seen observed between neighboring powers."

This remark was received with general laughter and applause. During the tumult, Morok questioned one of the waiters, and then exclaimed in a shrill tone, which rose above the clamor: "I demand a hearing!"

"Granted!" cried the others, gayly. During the silence which followed the exclamation of Morok, the noise was again heard; it was this time quicker than before.

"The lodger is innocent," said Morok, with a strange smile, "and would be quite incapable of interfering with your enjoyment."

"Then why does he keep up that knocking?" said Ninny Moulin, emptying his glass.

"Like a deaf man who has lost his ear-horn?" added the young artist.

"It is not the lodger who is knocking" said Morok, in a sharp, quick tone; "for they are nailing him down in his coffin." A sudden and mournful silence followed these words.

"His coffin no, I am wrong," resumed Morok; "her coffin, I should say, or more properly their coffin; for, in these pressing times, they put mother and child together."

"A woman!" cried PLEASURE, addressing the writer; "is it a woman that is dead?"

"Yes, ma'am; a poor young woman about twenty years of age," answered the waiter in a sorrowful tone. "Her little girl, that she was nursing, died soon after—all in less than two hours. My master is very sorry that you ladies and gents should be disturbed in this way; but he could not foresee this misfortune, as yesterday morning the young woman was quite well, and singing with all her might—no one could have been gayer than she was."

Upon these words, it was as if a funeral pall had been suddenly thrown over a scene lately so full of joy; all the rubicund and jovial faces took an expression of sadness; no one had the hardihood to make a jest of mother and child, nailed down together in the same coffin. The silence became so profound, that one could hear each breath oppressed by terror: the last blows of the hammer seemed to strike painfully on every heart; it appeared as if each sad feeling, until now repressed, was about to replace that animation and gayety, which had been more factitious than sincere. The moment was decisive. It was necessary to strike an immediate blow, and to raise the spirits of the guests, for many pretty rosy faces began to grow pale, many scarlet ears became suddenly white; Ninny Moulin's were of the number.

On the contrary, Sleepinbuff exhibited an increase of audacity; he drew up his figure, bent down from the effects of exhaustion, and, with a cheek slightly flushed, he exclaimed: "Well, waiter? are those bottles of brandy coming? And the punch? Devil and all! are the dead to frighten the living?"

"He's right! Down with sorrow, and let's have the punch!" cried several of the guests, who felt the necessity of reviving their courage.

"Forward, punch!"

"Begone, dull care!"

"Jollity forever!"

"Gentlemen, here is the punch," said a waiter, opening the door. At sight of the flaming beverage, which was to reanimate their enfeebled spirits, the room rang with the loudest applause.

The sun had just set. The room was large, being capable of dining a hundred guests; and the windows were few, narrow, and half veiled by red cotton curtains. Though it was not yet night, some portions of this vast saloon were almost entirely dark. Two waiters brought the monster-punch, in an immense brass kettle, brilliant as gold, suspended from an iron bar, and crowned with flames of changing color. The burning beverage was then placed upon the table, to the great joy of the guests, who began to forget their past alarms.

"Now," said Jacques to Morok, in a taunting tone, "while the punch is burning, we will have our duel. The company shall judge." Then, pointing to the two bottles of brandy, which the waiter had brought, Jacques added: "Choose your weapon!"

"Do you choose," answered Morok.

"Well! here's your bottle—and here's your glass. Ninny Moulin shall be umpire."

"I do not refuse to be judge of the field," answered the religious writer, "only I must warn you, comrade, that you are playing a desperate game, and that just now, as one of these gentlemen has said, the neck of a bottle of brandy in one's mouth, is perhaps more dangerous than the barrel of a loaded pistol."

"Give the word, old fellow!" said Jacques, interrupting Ninny Moulin, "or I will give it myself."

"Since you will have it so—so be it!"

"The first who gives in is conquered," said Jacques.

"Agreed!" answered Morok.

"Come, gentlemen, attention! we must follow every movement," resumed Ninny Moulin. "Let us first see if the bottles are of the same size—equality of weapons being the foremost condition."

During these preparations, profound silence reigned in the room. The courage of the majority of those present, animated for a moment by the arrival of the punch, was soon again depressed by gloomy thoughts, as they vaguely foresaw the danger of the contest between Morok and Jacques. This impression joined to the sad thoughts occasioned by the incident of the coffin, darkened by degrees many a countenance. Some of the guests, indeed, continued to make a show of rejoicing, but their gayety appeared forced. Under certain circumstances, the smallest things will have the most powerful effect. We have said that, after sunset, a portion of this large room was plunged in obscurity; therefore, the guests who sat in the remote corners of the apartment, had no other light than the reflection of the flaming punch. Now it is well known, that the flame of burning spirit throws a livid, bluish tint over the countenance; it was therefore a strange, almost frightful spectacle, to see a number of the guests, who happened to be at a distance from the windows, in this ghastly and fantastic light.

The painter, more struck than all the rest by this effect of color, exclaimed: "Look! at this end of the table, we might fancy ourselves feasting with cholera-patients, we are such fine blues and greens."

This jest was not much relished. Fortunately, the loud voice of Ninny Moulin demanded attention, and for a moment turned the thoughts of the company.

"The lists are open," cried the religious writer, really more frightened than he chose to appear. "Are you ready, brave champions?" he added.

"We are ready," said Morok and Jacques.

"Present! fire!" cried Ninny Moulin, clapping his hands. And the two drinkers each emptied a tumbler full of brandy at a draught.

Morok did not even knit his brow; his marble face remained impassible; with a steady hand he replaced his glass upon the table. But Jacques, as he put down his glass, could not conceal a slight convulsive trembling, caused by internal suffering.

"Bravely done!" cried Ninny Moulin. "The quarter of a bottle of brandy at a draught—it is glorious! No one else here would be capable of such prowess. And now, worthy champions, if you believe me, you will stop where you are."

"Give the word!" answered Jacques, intrepidly. And, with feverish and shaking hand, he seized the bottle; then suddenly, instead of filling his glass, he said to Morok: "Bah! we want no glasses. It is braver to drink from the bottle. I dare you to it!"

Morok's only answer was to shrug his shoulders, and raise the neck of the bottle to his lips. Jacques hastened to imitate him. The thin, yellowish, transparent glass gave a perfect view of the progressive diminution of the liquor. The stony countenance of Morok, and the pale thin face of Jacques, on which already stood large drops of cold sweat, were now, as well as the features of the other guests, illuminated by the bluish light of the punch; every eye was fixed upon Morok and Jacques, with that barbarous curiosity which cruel spectacles seem involuntarily to inspire.

Jacques continued to drink, holding the bottle in his left hand; suddenly, he closed and tightened the fingers of his right hand with a convulsive movement; his hair clung to his icy forehead, and his countenance revealed an agony of pain. Yet he continued to drink; only, without removing his lips from the neck of the bottle, he lowered it for an instant, as if to recover breath. Just then, Jacques met the sardonic look of Morok, who continued to drink with his accustomed impassibility. Thinking that he saw the expression of insulting triumph in Morok's glance, Jacques raised his elbow abruptly, and drank with avidity a few drops more. But his strength was exhausted. A quenchless fire devoured his vitals. His sufferings were too intense, and he could no longer bear up against them. His head fell backwards, his jaws closed convulsively, he crushed the neck of the bottle between his teeth, his neck grew rigid, his limbs writhed with spasmodic action, and he became almost senseless.

"Jacques, my good fellow! it is nothing," cried Morok, whose ferocious glance now sparkled with diabolical joy. Then, replacing his bottle on the table, he rose to go to the aid of Ninny Moulin, who was vainly endeavoring to hold Sleepinbuff.

This sudden attack had none of the symptoms of cholera. Yet terror seized upon all present; one of the women was taken with hysterics, and another uttered piercing cries and fainted away. Ninny Moulin, leaving Jacques in the hands of Morok, ran towards the door to seek for help,—when that door was suddenly opened, and the religious writer drew back in alarm, at the sight of the unexpected personage who appeared on the threshold.

CHAPTER XXII.

MEMORIES.

The person before whom Ninny Moulin stopped in such extreme astonishment was the Bacchanal Queen.

Pale and wan, with, hair in disorder, hollow cheeks, sunken eyes, and clothed almost in rags, this brilliant and joyous heroine of so many mad orgies was now only the shadow of her former self. Misery and grief were impressed on that countenance, once so charming. Hardly had she entered the room, when Cephyse paused; her mournful and unquiet gaze strove to penetrate the half-obscurity of the apartment, in search of him she longed to see. Suddenly the girl started, and uttered a loud scream. She had just perceived, at the other side of a long table, by the bluish light of the punch, Jacques struggling with Morok and one of the guests, who were hardly able to restrain his convulsive movements.

At this sight Cephyse, in her first alarm, carried away by her affection, did what she had so often done in the intoxication of joy and pleasure. Light and agile, instead of losing precious time in making a long circuit, she sprang at once upon the table, passed nimbly through the array of plates and bottles, and with one spring was by the side of the sufferer.

"Jacques!" she exclaimed, without yet remarking the lion-tamer, and throwing herself on the neck of her lover. "Jacques! it is I—Cephyse!"

That well-known voice, that heart-piercing cry, which came from the bottom of the soul, seemed not unheard by Sleepinbuff. He turned his head mechanically towards the Bacchanal Queen, without opening his eyes, and heaved a deep sigh; his stiffened limbs relaxed, a slight trembling succeeded to the convulsions, and in a few seconds his heavy eyelids were raised with an effort, so as to uncover his dull and wandering gaze. Mute with astonishment, the spectators of this scene felt an uneasy curiosity. Cephyse, kneeling beside her lover, bathed his hands in her tears, covered them with kisses, and exclaimed, in a voice broken by sobs, "It is I—Cephyse—I have found you again—it was not my fault that I abandoned you! Forgive me, forgive—"

"Wretched woman!" cried Morok, irritated at this meeting, which might, perhaps, be fatal to his projects; "do you wish to kill him? In his present state, this agitation is death. Begone!" So saying, he seized Cephyse suddenly by the arm, just as Jacques, waking, as it were, from a painful dream, began to distinguish what was passing around him.

"You! It is you!" cried the Bacchanal Queen, in amazement, as she recognized Morok, "who separated me from Jacques!"

She paused; for the dim eye of the victim, as it rested upon her, grew suddenly bright.

"Cephyse!" murmured Jacques; "is it you?"

"Yes, it is I," answered she, in a voice of deep emotion; "who have come—I will tell you—"

She was unable to continue, and, as she clasped her hands together, her pale, agitated, tearful countenance expressed her astonishment and despair at the mortal change which had taken place in the features of Jacques. He understood the cause of her surprise, and as he contemplated, in his turn, the suffering and emaciated countenance of Cephyse, he said to her, "Poor girl! you also have had to bear much grief, much misery—I should hardly have known you."

"Yes," replied Cephyse, "much grief—much misery—and worse than misery," she added, trembling, whilst a deep blush overspread her pale features.

"Worse than misery?" said Jacques, astonished.

"But it is you who have suffered," hastily resumed Cephyse, without answering her lover.

"Just now, I was going to make an end of it—your voice has recalled me for an instant—but I feel something here," and he laid his hand upon his breast, "which never gives quarter. It is all the same now—I have seen you—I shall die happy."

"You shall not die, Jacques; I am here—"

"Listen to one, my girl. If I had a bushel of live coal in my stomach, it could hardly burn me more. For more than a month, I have been consuming my body by a slow fire. This gentleman," he added, glancing at Morok, "this dear friend, always undertook to feed the flame. I do not regret life; I have lost the habit of work, and taken to drink and riot; I should have finished by becoming a thorough blackguard: I preferred that my friend here should amuse himself with lighting a furnace in my inside. Since what I drank just now, I am certain that it fumes like yonder punch."

"You are both foolish and ungrateful," said Morok, shrugging his shoulders; "you held out your glass, and I filled it—and, faith, we shall drink long and often together yet."

For some moments, Cephyse had not withdrawn her eyes from Morok. "I tell you, that you have long blown the fire, in which I have burnt my skin," resumed Jacques, addressing Morok in a feeble voice, "so that they may not think I die of cholera. It would look as if I had been frightened by the part I played. I do not therefore reproach you, my affectionate friend," added he, with a sardonic smile; "you dug my grave gayly—and sometimes, when, seeing the great dark hole, into which I was about to fall, I drew back a step—but you, my excellent friend, still pushed me forward, saying, 'Go on, my boy, go on!'—and I went on—and here I am—"

So saying, Sleepinbuff burst into a bitter laugh, which sent an icy shudder through the spectators of this scene.

"My good fellow," said Morok, coolly, "listen to me, and follow my advice."

"Thank you! I know your advice—and, instead of listening to you, I prefer speaking to my poor Cephyse. Before I go down to the moles, I should like to tell her what weighs on my heart."

"Jacques," replied Cephyse, "do not talk so. I tell you, you shall not die."

"Why, then, my brave Cephyse, I shall owe my life to you," returned Jacques, in a tone of serious feeling, which surprised the spectators. "Yes," resumed he, "when I came to myself, and saw you so poorly clad, I felt something good about my heart—do you know why?—it was because I said to myself, 'Poor girl! she has kept her word bravely; she has chosen to toil, and want, and suffer—rather than take another love—who would have given her what I gave her as long as I could'—and that thought, Cephyse, refreshed my soul. I needed it, for I was burning—and I burn still," added he, clinching his fists with pain; "but that made me happy—it did me good—thanks, my good, brave Cephyse—yes, you are good and brave—and you were right; for I never loved any but you in the wide world; and if, in my degradation, I had one thought that raised me a little above the filth, and made me regret that I was not better—the thought was of you! Thanks then, my poor, dear love," said Jacques, whose hot and shining eyes were becoming moist; "thanks once again," and he reached his cold hand to Cephyse; "if I die, I shall die happy—if I live, I shall live happy also. Give me your hand, my brave Cephyse!—you have acted like a good and honest creature."

Instead of taking the hand which Jacques offered her, Cephyse, still kneeling, bowed her head, and dared not raise her eyes to her lover.

"You don't answer," said he, leaning over towards the young girl; "you don't take my hand—why is this?"

The unfortunate creature only answered by stifled sobs. Borne down with shame, she held herself in so humble, so supplicating an attitude, that her forehead almost touched the feet of her lover.

Amazed at the silence and conduct of the Bacchanal Queen, Jacques looked at her with increasing agitation; suddenly he stammered out with trembling lips, "Cephyse, I know you. If you do not take my hand, it is because—"

Then, his voice failing, he added, in a dull tone, after a moment's silence, "When, six weeks ago, I was taken to prison, did you not say to me, 'Jacques, I swear that I will work—and if need be, live in horrible misery—but I will live true!' That was your promise. Now, I know you never speak false; tell me you have kept your word, and I shall believe you."

Cephyse only answered by a heart-rending sob, as she pressed the knees of Jacques against her heaving bosom. By a strange contradiction, more common than is generally thought—this man, degraded by intoxication and debauchery, who, since he came out of prison, had plunged in every excess, and tamely yielded to all the fatal incitements of Morok, yet received a fearful blow, when he learned, by the mute avowal of Cephyse, the infidelity, of this creature, whom he had loved in spite of degradation. The first impulse of Jacques was terrible. Notwithstanding his weakness and exhaustion, he succeeded in rising from his seat, and, with a countenance contracted by rage and despair, he seized a knife, before they had time to prevent him, and turned it upon Cephyse. But at the moment he was about to strike, shrinking from an act of murder, he hurled the knife far away from him, and falling back into the chair, covered his face with his hands.

At the cry of Ninny Moulin, who had, though late, thrown himself upon Jacques to take away the knife, Cephyse raised her head: Jacques's woeful dejection wrung her heart; she rose, and fell upon his neck, notwithstanding his resistance, exclaiming in a voice broken by sobs, "Jacques, if you knew! if you only knew—listen—do not condemn me without hearing me—I will tell you all, I swear to you—without falsehood—this man," and she pointed to Morok, "will not dare deny what I say; he came, and told me to have the courage to—"

"I do not reproach you. I have no right to reproach you. Let me die in peace. I ask nothing but that now," said Jacques, in a still weaker voice, as he repulsed Cephyse. Then he added, with a grievous and bitter smile, "Luckily, I have my dose. I knew—what I was doing—when I accepted the duel with brandy."

"No, you shall not die, and you shall hear me," cried Cephyse, with a bewildered air; "you shall hear me, and everybody else shall hear me. They shall see that it is not my fault. Is it not so, gentlemen? Do I not deserve pity? You will entreat Jacques to forgive me; for if driven by misery—finding no work—I was forced to this—not for the sake of any luxury—you see the rags I wear—but to get bread and shelter for my poor, sick sister—dying, and even more miserable than myself—would you not have pity upon me? Do you think one finds pleasure in one's infamy?" cried the unfortunate, with a burst of frightful laughter; then she added, in a low voice, and with a shudder, "Oh, if you knew, Jacques! it is so infamous, so horrible, that I preferred death to falling so low a second time. I should have killed myself, had I not heard you were here." Then, seeing that Jacques did not answer her, but shook his head mournfully as he sank down though still supported by Ninny Moulin, Cephyse exclaimed, as she lifted her clasped hands towards him, "Jacques! one word—for pity's sake—forgive me!"

"Gentlemen, pray remove this woman," cried Morok; "the sight of her causes my friend too painful emotions."

"Come, my dear child, be reasonable," said several of the guests, who, deeply moved by this scene, were endeavoring to withdraw Cephyse from it; "leave him, and come with us; he is not in any danger."

"Gentlemen! oh, gentlemen!" cried the unfortunate creature, bursting into tears, and raising her hands in supplication; "listen to me—I will do all that you wish me—I will go—but, in heaven's name, send for help, and do not let him die thus. Look, what pain he suffers! what horrible convulsions!"

"She is right," said one of the guests, hastening towards the door; "we must send for a doctor."

"There is no doctor to be found," said another; "they are all too busy."

"We will do better than that," cried a third; "the Hospital is just opposite, and we can carry the poor fellow thither. They will give him instant help. A leaf of the table will make a litter, and the table cloth a covering."

"Yes, yes, that is it," said several voices; "let us carry him over at once."

Jacques, burnt up with brandy, and overcome by his interview with Cephyse, had again fallen into violent convulsions. It was the dying paroxysm of the unfortunate man. They were obliged to tie him with the ends of the cloth, so as to secure him to the leaf which was to serve for a litter, which two of the guests hastened to carry away. They yielded to the supplication of Cephyse, who asked, as a last favor, to accompany Jacques to the Hospital. When the mournful procession quitted the great room of the eating-house, there was a general flight among the guests. Men and women made haste to wrap themselves in their cloaks, in order to conceal their costumes. The coaches, which had been ordered in tolerable number for the return of the masquerade, had luckily arrived. The defiance had been fully carried out, the audacious bravado accomplished, and they could now retire with the honors of war. Whilst a part of the guests were still in the room, an uproar, at first distant, but which soon drew nearer, broke out with incredible fury in the square of Notre Dame.

Jacques had been carried to the outer door of the tavern. Morok and Ninny Moulin, striving to open a passage through the crowd in the direction of the Hospital, preceded the litter. A violent reflux of the multitude soon forced them to stop, whilst a new storm of savage outcries burst from the other extremity of the square, near the angle of the church.

"What is it then?" asked Ninny Moulin of one of those ignoble figures that was leaping up before him. "What are those cries?"

"They are making mince-meat of a poisoner, like him they have thrown into the river," replied the man. "If you want to see the fun, follow me close," added he, "and peg away with your elbows, for fear you should be too late."

Hardly had the wretch pronounced these words than a dreadful shriek sounded above the roar of the crowd, through which the bearers of the litter, preceded by Morok, were with difficulty making their way. It was Cephyse who uttered that cry. Jacques (one of the seven heirs of the Rennepont family) had just expired in her arms! By a strange fatality, at the very moment that the despairing exclamation of Cephyse announced that death, another cry rose from that part of the square where they were attacking the poisoner. That distant, supplicating cry, tremulous with horrible alarm, like the last appeal of a man staggering beneath the blows of his murderers, chilled the soul of Morok in the midst of his execrable triumph.

"Damnation!" cried the skillful assassin, who had selected drunkenness and debauchery for his murderous but legal weapons; "it is the voice of the Abbe d'Aigrigny, whom they have in their clutches!"

CHAPTER XXIII.

THE POISONER.

It is necessary to go back a little before relating the adventure of Father d'Aigrigny, whose cry of distress made so deep an impression upon Morok just at the moment of Jacques Rennepont's death. We have said that the most absurd and alarming reports were circulating in Paris; not only did people talk of poison given to the sick or thrown into the public fountains, but it was also said that wretches had been surprised in the act of putting arsenic into the pots which are usually kept all ready on the counters of wine-shops. Goliath was on his way to rejoin Morok, after delivering a message to Father d'Aigrigny, who was waiting in a house on the Place de l'Archeveche. He entered a wine-shop in the Rue de la Calandre, to get some refreshment, and having drunk two glasses of wine, he proceeded to pay for them. Whilst the woman of the house was looking for change, Goliath, mechanically and very innocently, rested his hand on the mouth of one of the pots that happened to be within his reach.

The tall stature of this man and his repulsive and savage countenance had already alarmed the good woman, whose fears and prejudices had previously been roused by the public rumors on the subject of poisoning; but when she saw Goliath place his hand over the mouth of one of her pots, she cried out in dismay: "Oh! my gracious! what are you throwing into that pot?" At these words, spoken in a loud voice, and with the accent of terror, two or three of the drinkers at one of the tables rose precipitately, and ran to the counter, while one of them rashly exclaimed: "It is a poisoner!"

Goliath, not aware of the reports circulated in the neighborhood, did not at first understand of what he was accused. The men raised their voices as they called on him to answer the charge; but he, trusting to his strength, shrugged his shoulders in disdain, and roughly demanded the change, which the pale and frightened hostess no longer thought of giving him.

"Rascal!" cried one of the men, with so much violence that several of the passers-by stopped to listen; "you shall have your change when you tell us what you threw in the pot!"

"Ha! did he throw anything into the wine-pot?" said one of the passers by.

"It is, perhaps, a poisoner," said another.

"He ought to be taken up," added a third.

"Yes, yes," cried those in the house—honest people perhaps, but under the influence of the general panic; "he must be taken up, for he has been throwing poison into the wine-pots."

The words "He is a poisoner" soon spread through the group, which, at first composed of three or four persons, increased every instant around the door of the wine-shop. A dull, menacing clamor began to rise from the crowd; the first accuser, seeing his fears thus shared and almost justified, thought he was acting like a good and courageous citizen in taking Goliath by the collar, and saying to him: "Come and explain yourself at the guard-house, villain!"

The giant, already provoked at insults of which he did not perceive the real meaning, was exasperated at this sudden attack; yielding to his natural brutality, he knocked his adversary down upon the counter, and began to hammer him with his fists. During this collision, several bottles and two or three panes of glass were broken with much noise, whilst the woman of the house, more and more frightened, cried out with all her might; "Help! a poisoner! Help! murder!"

At the sound of the breaking windows and these cries of distress, the passers-by, of whom the greater number believed in the stories about the poisoners, rushed into the shop to aid in securing Goliath. But the latter, thanks to his herculean strength, after struggling for some moments with seven or eight persons, knocked down two of his most furious assailants, disengaged himself from the others, drew near the counter, and, taking a vigorous spring, rushed head-foremost, like a bull about to butt, upon the crowd that blocked up the door; then, forcing a passage, by the help of his enormous shoulders and athletic arms, he made his way into the street, and ran with all speed in the direction of the square of Notre-Dame, his garments torn, his head bare, and his countenance pale and full of rage. Immediately, a number of persons from amongst the crowd started in pursuit of Goliath, and a hundred voices exclaimed: "Stop—stop the poisoner!"

Hearing these cries, and seeing a man draw near with a wild and troubled look, a butcher, who happened to be passing with his large, empty tray on his head, threw it against Goliath's shins, and taken by surprise, he stumbled and fell. The butcher, thinking he had performed as heroic an action as if he had encountered a mad dog, flung himself on Goliath, and rolled over with him on the pavement, exclaiming: "Help! it is a poisoner! Help! help!" This scene took place not far from the Cathedral, but at some distance from the crowd which was pressing round the hospital gate, as well as from the eating-house in which the masquerade of the cholera then was. The day was now drawing to a close. On the piercing call of the butcher, several groups, at the head of which were Ciboule and the quarryman, flew towards the scene of the struggle, while those who had pursued the pretended poisoner from the Rue de la Calandre, reached the square on their side.

At sight of this threatening crowd advancing towards him, Goliath, whilst he continued to defend himself against the butcher, who held him with the tenacity of a bull-dog, felt that he was lost unless he could rid himself of this adversary before the arrival of the rest; with a furious blow of the fist, therefore, he broke the jaw of the butcher, who just then was above him, and disengaging himself from his hold, he rose, and staggered a few steps forward. Suddenly he stopped. He saw that he was surrounded. Behind him rose the walls of the cathedral; to the right and left, and in front of him, advanced a hostile multitude. The groans uttered by the butcher, who had just been lifted from the ground covered with blood, augmented the fury of the populace.

This was a terrible moment for Goliath: still standing alone in the centre of a ring that grew smaller every second, he saw on all sides angry enemies rushing towards him, and uttering cries of death. As the wild boar turns round once or twice, before resolving to stand at bay and face the devouring pack, Goliath, struck with terror, made one or two abrupt and wavering movements. Then, as he abandoned the possibility of flight, instinct told him that he had no mercy to expect from a crowd given up to blind and savage fury—a fury the more pitiless as it was believed to be legitimate. Goliath determined, therefore, at least to sell his life dearly; he sought for a knife in his pocket, but, not finding it, he threw out his left leg in an athletic posture, and holding up his muscular arms, hard and stiff as bars of iron, waited with intrepidity for the shock.

The first who approached Goliath was Ciboule. The hag, heated and out of breath, instead of rushing upon him, paused, stooped down, and taking off one of the large wooden shoes that she wore, hurled it at the giant's head with so much force and with so true an aim that it struck him right in the eye, which hung half out of its socket. Goliath pressed his hands to his face, and uttered a cry of excruciating pain.

"I've made him squint!" said Ciboule, with a burst of laughter.

Goliath, maddened by the pain, instead of waiting for the attack, which the mob still hesitated to begin, so greatly were they awed by his appearance of herculean strength—the only adversary worthy to cope with him being the quarryman, who had been borne to a distance by the surging of the crowd—Goliath, in his rage, rushed headlong upon the nearest. Such a struggle was too unequal to last long; but despair redoubled the Colossus's strength, and the combat was for a moment terrible. The unfortunate man did not fall at once. For some seconds, almost buried amid a swarm of furious assailants, one saw now his mighty arm rise and fall like a sledge hammer, beating upon skulls and faces, and now his enormous head, livid and bloody, drawn back by some of the combatants hanging to his tangled hair. Here and there sudden openings and violent oscillations of the crowd bore witness to the incredible energy of Goliath's defence. But when the quarryman succeeded in reaching him, Goliath was overpowered and thrown down. A long, savage cheer in triumph announced this fall; for, under such circumstances, to "go under" is "to die." Instantly a thousand breathless and angry voices repeated the cry of "Death to the poisoner!"

Then began one of those scenes of massacre and torture, worthy of cannibals, horrible to relate, and the more incredible, that they happen almost always in the presence, and often with the aid, of honest and humane people, who, blinded by false notions and stupid prejudices, allow themselves to be led into all sorts of barbarity, under the idea of performing an act of inexorable justice. As it frequently happens, the sight of the blood which flowed in torrents from Goliath's wounds inflamed to madness the rage of his assailants. A hundred fists struck at the unhappy man; he was stamped under foot, his face and chest were beaten in. Ever and anon, in the midst of furious cries of "Death to the poisoner!" heavy blows were audible, followed by stifled groans. It was a frightful butchery. Each individual, yielding to a sanguinary frenzy, came in turn to strike his blow; or to tear off his morsel of flesh. Women—yes, women—mothers!—came to spend their rage on this mutilated form.

There was one moment of frightful terror. With his face all bruised and covered with mud, his garments in rags, his chest bare, red, gaping with wounds—Goliath, availing himself of a moment's weariness on the part of his assassins, who believed him already, finished, succeeded, by one of those convulsive starts frequent in the last agony, in raising himself to his feet for a few seconds; then, blind with wounds and loss of blood, striking about his arms in the air as if to parry blows that were no longer struck, he muttered these words, which came from his mouth, accompanied by a crimson torrent: "Mercy! I am no poisoner. Mercy!" This sort of resurrection produced so great an effect on the crowd, that for an instant they fell hack affrighted. The clamor ceased, and a small space was left around the victim. Some hearts began even to feel pity; when the quarryman, seeing Goliath blinded with blood, groping before him with his hands, exclaimed in ferocious allusion to a well-known game: "Now for blind-man's-bluff."

Then, with a violent kick, he again threw down the victim, whose head struck twice heavily on the pavement.

Just as the giant fell a voice from amongst the crowd exclaimed: "It is Goliath! stop! he is innocent."

It was Father d'Aigrigny, who, yielding to a generous impulse, was making violent efforts to reach the foremost rank of the actors in this scene, and who cried out, as he came nearer, pale, indignant, menacing: "You are cowards and murderers! This man is innocent. I know him. You shall answer for his life."

These vehement words were received with loud murmurs.

"You know that poisoner," cried the quarryman, seizing the Jesuit by the collar; "then perhaps you are a poisoner too.

"Wretch," exclaimed Father d'Aigrigny, endeavoring to shake himself loose from the grasp, "do you dare to lay hand upon me?"

"Yes, I dare do anything," answered the quarryman.

"He knows him: he's a poisoner like the other," cried the crowd, pressing round the two adversaries; whilst Goliath, who had fractured his skull in the fall, uttered a long death-rattle.

At a sudden movement of Father d'Aigrigny, who disengaged himself from the quarryman, a large glass phial of peculiar form, very thick, and filled with a greenish liquor, fell from his pocket, and rolled close to the dying Goliath. At sight of this phial, many voices exclaimed together: "It is poison! Only see! He had poison upon him."

The clamor redoubled at this accusation, and they pressed so close to Abbe d'Aigrigny, that he exclaimed: "Do not touch me! do not approach me!"

"If he is a poisoner," said a voice, "no more mercy for him than for the other."

"I a poisoner?" said the abbe, struck with horror.

Ciboule had darted upon the phial; the quarryman seized it from her, uncorked it and presenting it to Father d'Aigrigny, said to him: "Now tell us what is that?"

"It is not poison," cried Father d'Aigrigny.

"Then drink it!" returned the quarryman.

"Yes, yes! let him drink it!" cried the mob.

"Never," answered Father d'Aigrigny, in extreme alarm. And he drew back as he spoke, pushing away the phial with his hand.

"Do you see? It is poison. He dares not drink it," they exclaimed. Hemmed in on every side, Father d'Aigrigny stumbled against the body of Goliath.

"My friends," cried the Jesuit, who, without being a poisoner, found himself exposed to a terrible alternative, for his phial contained aromatic salts of extraordinary strength, designed for a preservative against the cholera, and as dangerous to swallow as any poison, "my good friends, you are in error. I conjure you, in the name of heaven—"

"If that is not poison, drink it!" interrupted the quarryman, as he again offered the bottle to the Jesuit.

"If he does not drink it, death to the poisoner of the poor!"

"Yes!—death to him! death to him!"

"Unhappy men!" cried Father d'Aigrigny, whilst his hair stood on end with terror; "do you mean to murder me?"

"What about all those, that you and your mate have killed, you wretch?"

"But it is not true—and—"

"Drink, then!" repeated the inflexible quarryman; "I ask you for the last time."

"To drink that would be death," cried Father d'Aigrigny.

"Oh! only hear the wretch!" cried the mob, pressing closer to him; "he has confessed—he has confessed!"

"He has betrayed himself!"[40]

"He said, 'to drink that would be death!'"

"But listen to me," cried the abbe, clasping his hands together; "this phial is—"

Furious cries interrupted Father d'Aigrigny. "Ciboule, make an end of that one!" cried the quarryman, spurning Goliath with his foot. "I will begin this one!" And he seized Father d'Aigrigny by the throat.

At these words, two different groups formed themselves. One, led by Ciboule, "made an end" of Goliath, with kicks and blows, stones and wooden shoes; his body was soon reduced to a horrible thing, mutilated, nameless, formless—a mere inert mass of filth and mangled flesh. Ciboule gave her cloak, which they tied to one of the dislocated ankles of the body, and thus dragged it to the parapet of the quay. There, with shouts of ferocious joy, they precipitated the bloody remains into the river. Now who does not shudder at the thought that, in a time of popular commotion, a word, a single word, spoken imprudently, even by an honest man, and without hatred, will suffice to provoke so horrible a murder.

"Perhaps it is a poisoner!" said one of the drinkers in the tavern of the Rue de la Calandre—nothing more—and Goliath had been pitilessly murdered.

What imperious reasons for penetrating the lowest depths of the masses with instruction and with light—to enable unfortunate creatures to defend themselves from so many stupid prejudices, so many fatal superstitions, so much implacable fanaticism!—How can we ask for calmness, reflection, self-control, or the sentiment of justice from abandoned beings, whom ignorance has brutalized, and misery depraved, and suffering made ferocious, and of whom society takes no thought, except when it chains them to the galleys, or binds them ready for the executioner! The terrible cry which had so startled Morok was uttered by Father d'Aigrigny as the quarryman laid his formidable hand upon him, saying to Ciboule: "Make an end of that one—I will begin this one!"

[40] This fact is historical. A man was murdered because a phial full of ammonia was found upon him. On his refusal to drink it, the populace, persuaded that the bottle contained poison, tore him to pieces.

CHAPTER XXIV.

IN THE CATHEDRAL.

Night was almost come, as the mutilated body of Goliath was thrown into the river. The oscillations of the mob had carried into the street, which runs along the left side of the cathedral, the group into whose power Father d'Aigrigny had fallen. Having succeeded in freeing himself from the grasp of the quarryman, but still closely pressed by the multitude that surrounded him, crying, "Death to the poisoner!" he retreated step by step, trying to parry the blows that were dealt him. By presence of mind, address, and courage, recovering at that critical moment his old military energy, he had hitherto been able to resist and to remain firm on his feet—knowing, by the example of Goliath, that to fall was to die. Though he had little hope of being heard to any purpose, the abbe continued to call for help with all his might. Disputing the ground inch by inch, he manoeuvred so as to draw near one of the lateral walls of the church, and at length succeeded in ensconcing himself in a corner formed by the projection of a buttress, and close by a little door.

This position was rather favorable. Leaning with his back against the wall, Father d'Aigrigny was sheltered from the attacks of a portion of his assailants. But the quarryman, wishing to deprive him of this last chance of safety, rushed upon him, with the intention of dragging him out into the circle where he would have been trampled under foot. The fear of death gave Father d'Aigrigny extraordinary strength, and he was able once more to repulse the quarryman, and remain entrenched in the corner where he had taken refuge. The resistance of the victim redoubled the rage of the assailants. Cries of murderous import resounded with new violence. The quarryman again rushed upon Father d'Aigrigny, saying, "Follow me, friends! this lasts too long. Let us make an end of it."

Father d'Aigrigny saw that he was lost. His strength was exhausted, and he felt himself sinking; his legs trembled under him, and a cloud obscured his sight; the howling of the furious mob began to sound dull upon his ear. The effects of violent contusions, received during the struggle, both on the head and chest, were now very perceptible. Two or three times, a mixture of blood and foam rose to the lips of the abbe; his position was a desperate one.

"To be slaughtered by these brutes, after escaping death so often in war!" Such was the thought of Father d'Aigrigny, as the quarryman rushed upon him.

Suddenly, at the very moment when the abbe, yielding to the instinct of self-preservation, uttered one last call for help, in a heart-piercing voice, the door against which he leaned opened behind him, and a firm hand caught hold of him, and pulled him into the church. Thanks to this movement, performed with the rapidity of lightning, the quarryman, thrown forward in his attempt to seize Father d'Aigrigny, could not check his progress, and found himself just opposite to the person who had come, as it were, to take the place of the victim.

The quarryman stopped short, and then fell back a couple of paces, so much was he amazed at this sudden apparition, and impressed, like the rest of the crowd, with a vague feeling of admiration and respect at sight of him who had come so miraculously to the aid of Father d'Aigrigny. It was Gabriel. The young missionary remained standing on the threshold of the door. His long black cassock was half lost in the shadows of the cathedral; whilst his angelic countenance, with its border of long light hair, now pale and agitated by pity and grief, was illumined by the last faint rays of twilight. This countenance shone with so divine a beauty, and expressed such touching and tender compassion, that the crowd felt awed as, with his large blue eyes full of tears, and his hands clasped together, he exclaimed, in a sonorous voice: "Have mercy, my brethren! Be humane—be just!"

Recovering from his first feeling of surprise and involuntary emotion, the quarryman advanced a step towards Gabriel, and said to him: "No mercy for the poisoner! we must have him! Give him up to us, or we go and take him!"

"You cannot think of it, my brethren," answered Gabriel; "the church is a sacred place—a place of refuge for the persecuted."

"We would drag our prisoner from the altar!" answered the quarryman, roughly; "so give him up to us."

"Listen to me, my brethren," said Gabriel, extending his arms towards them.

"Down with the shaveling!" cried the quarryman; "let us go in and hunt him up in the church!"

"Yes, yes!" cried the mob, again led away by the violence of this wretch, "down with the black gown!"

"They are all of a piece!"

"Down with them!"

"Let us do as we did at the archbishop's!"

"Or at Saint-Germain-l'Auxerrois!"

"What do our likes care for a church?"

"If the priests defend the poisoners, we'll pitch them into the water too!"

"Yes, yes!"

"I'll show you the lead!" cried the quarryman; and followed by Ciboule, and a good number of determined men, he rushed towards Gabriel.

The missionary, who for some moments had watched the increasing fury of the crowd, had foreseen this movement; hastily retreating into the church, he succeeded, in spite of the efforts of the assailants, in nearly closing the door, and in barricading it by the help of a wooden bar, which he held in such a manner as would enable the door to resist for a few minutes.

Whilst he thus defended the entrance, Gabriel shouted to Father d'Aigrigny: "Fly, father! fly through the vestry! the other doors are fastened."

The Jesuit, overpowered by fatigue, covered with contusions, bathed in cold sweat, feeling his strength altogether fail, and too soon fancying himself in safety, had sunk, half fainting, into a chair. At the voice of Gabriel, he rose with difficulty, and, with a trembling step, endeavored to reach the choir, separated from the rest of the church by an iron railing.

"Quick, father!" added Gabriel, in alarm, using every effort to maintain the door, which was now vigorously assailed. "Make haste! In a few minutes it will be too late. All alone!" continued the missionary, in despair, "alone, to arrest the progress of these madmen!"

He was indeed alone. At the first outbreak of the attack, three or four sacristans and other members of the establishment were in the church; but, struck with terror, and remembering the sack of the archbishop's palace, and of Saint-Germain-l'Auxerrois, they had immediately taken flight. Some of them had concealed themselves in the organ-loft and others fled into the vestry, the doors of which they locked after them, thus cutting off the retreat of Gabriel and Father d'Aigrigny. The latter, bent double by pain, yet roused by the missionary's portentive warning, helping himself on by means of the chairs he met with on his passage, made vain efforts to reach the choir railing. After advancing a few steps, vanquished by his suffering, he staggered and fell upon the pavement, deprived of sense and motion. At the same moment, Gabriel, in spite of the incredible energy with which the desire to save Father d'Aigrigny had inspired him, felt the door giving way beneath the formidable pressure from without.

Turning his head, to see if the Jesuit had at least quitted the church, Gabriel, to his great alarm, perceived that he was lying motionless at a few steps from the choir. To abandon the half-broken door, to run to Father d'Aigrigny, to lift him in his arms, and drag him within the railing of the choir, was for the young priest an action rapid as thought; for he closed the gate of the choir just at the instant that the quarryman and his band, having finished breaking down the door, rushed in a body into the church.

Standing in front of the choir, with his arms crossed upon his breast, Gabriel waited calmly and intrepidly for this mob, still more exasperated by such unexpected resistance.

The door once forced, the assailants rushed in with great violence. But hardly had they entered the church, than a strange scene took place. It was nearly dark; only a few silver lamps shed their pale light round the sanctuary, whose far outlines disappeared in the shadow. On suddenly entering the immense cathedral, dark, silent, and deserted, the most audacious were struck with awe, almost with fear in presence of the imposing grandeur of that stony solitude. Outcries and threats died away on the lips of the most furious. They seemed to dread awaking the echoes of those enormous arches, those black vaults, from which oozed a sepulchral dampness, which chilled their brows, inflamed with anger, and fell upon their shoulders like a mantle of ice.

Religious tradition, routine, habit, the memories of childhood, have so much influence upon men, that hardly had they entered the church, than several of the quarryman's followers respectfully took off their hats, bowed their bare heads, and walked along cautiously, as if to check the noise of their footsteps on the sounding stones. Then they exchanged a few words in a low and fearful whisper. Others timidly raised their eyes to the far heights of the topmost arches of that gigantic building, now lost in obscurity, and felt almost frightened to see themselves so little in the midst of that immensity of darkness. But at the first joke of the quarryman, who broke this respectful silence, the emotion soon passed away.

"Blood and thunder!" cried he; "are you fetching breath to sing vespers? If they had wine in the font, well and good!"

These words were received with a burst of savage laughter. "All this time the villain will escape!" said one.

"And we shall be done," added Ciboule.

"One would think we had cowards here, who are afraid of the sacristans!" cried the quarryman.

"Never!" replied the others in chorus; "we fear nobody."

"Forward!"

"Yes, yes—forward!" was repeated on all sides. And the animation, which had been calmed down for a moment, was redoubled in the midst of renewed tumult. Some moments after, the eyes of the assailants, becoming accustomed to the twilight, were able to distinguish in the midst of the faint halo shed around by a silver lamp, the imposing countenance of Gabriel, as he stood before the iron railing of the choir.

"The poisoner is here, hid in some corner," cried the quarryman. "We must force this parson to give us back the villain."

"He shall answer for him!"

"He took him into the church."

"He shall pay for both, if we do not find the other!"

As the first impression of involuntary respect was effaced from the minds of the crowd, their voices rose the louder, and their faces became the more savage and threatening, because they all felt ashamed of their momentary hesitation and weakness.

"Yes, yes!" cried many voices, trembling with rage, "we must have the life of one or the other!"

"Or of both!"

"So much the worse for this priest, if he wants to prevent us from serving out our poisoner!"

"Death to him! death to him!"

With this burst of ferocious yells, which were fearfully re-echoed from the groined arches of the cathedral, the mob, maddened by rage, rushed towards the choir, at the door of which Gabriel was standing. The young missionary, who, when placed on the cross by the savages of the Rocky Mountains, yet entreated heaven to spare his executioners, had too much courage in his heart, too much charity in his soul, not to risk his life a thousand times over to save Father d'Aigrigny's—the very man who had betrayed hire by such cowardly and cruel hypocrisy.

CHAPTER XXV.

THE MURDERERS.

The quarryman, followed by his gang, ran towards Gabriel, who had advanced a few paces from the choir-railing, and exclaimed, his eyes sparkling with rage: "Where is the poisoner? We will have him!"

"Who has told you, my brethren, that he is a poisoner?" replied Gabriel, with his deep, sonorous voice. "A poisoner! Where are the proofs—witnesses or victims?"

"Enough of that stuff! we are not here for confession," brutally answered the quarryman, advancing towards him in a threatening manner. "Give up the man to us; he shall be forthcoming, unless you choose to stand in his shoes?"

"Yes, yes!" exclaimed several voices; "they are 'in' with one another! One or the other we will have!"

"Very well, then; since it is so," said Gabriel, raising his head, and advancing with calmness, resignation; and fearlessness; "he or me," added he;—"it seems to make no difference to you—you are determined to have blood—take mine, and I will pardon you, my friends; for a fatal delusion has unsettled your reason."

These words of Gabriel, his courage, the nobleness of his attitude, the beauty of his countenance, had made an impression on some of the assailants, when suddenly a voice exclaimed: "Look! there is the poisoner, behind the railing!"

"Where—where?" cried they.

"There—don't you see?—stretched on the floor."

On hearing this, the mob, which had hitherto formed a compact mass, in the sort of passage separating the two sides of the nave, between the rows of chairs, dispersed in every direction, to reach the railing of the choir, the last and only barrier that now sheltered Father d'Aigrigny. During this manoeuvre the quarryman, Ciboule, and others, advanced towards Gabriel, exclaiming, with ferocious joy: "This time we have him. Death to the poisoner!"

To save Father d'Aigrigny, Gabriel would have allowed himself to be massacred at the entrance of the choir; but, a little further on, the railing, not above four feet in height, would in another instant be scaled or broken through. The Missionary lost all hope of saving the Jesuit from a frightful death. Yet he exclaimed: "Stop, poor deluded people!"—and, extending his arms, he threw himself in front of the crowd.

His words, gesture, and countenance, were expressive of an authority at once so affectionate and so fraternal, that there was a momentary hesitation amongst the mob. But to this hesitation soon succeeded the most furious cries of "Death; death!"

"You cry for his death?" cried Gabriel, growing still paler.

"Yes! yes!"

"Well, let him die," cried the missionary, inspired with a sudden thought; "let him die on the instant!"

These words of the young priest struck the crowd with amazement. For a few moments, they all stood mute, motionless, and as it were, paralyzed, looking at Gabriel in stupid astonishment.

"This man is guilty, you say," resumed the young missionary, in a voice trembling with emotion. "You have condemned him without proof, without witnesses—no matter, he must die. You reproach him with being a poisoner; where are his victims? You cannot tell—but no matter; he is condemned. You refuse to hear his defense, the sacred right of every accused person—no matter; the sentence is pronounced. You are at once his accusers, judges, and executioners. Be it so!—You have never seen till now this unfortunate man, he has done you no harm, he has perhaps not done harm to any one—yet you take upon yourselves the terrible responsibility of his death—understand me well—of his death. Be it so then! your conscience will absolve you—I will believe it. He must die; the sacredness of God's house will not save him—"

"No, no!" cried many furious voices.

"No," resumed Gabriel, with increasing warmth; "no you have determined to shed his blood, and you will shed it, even in the Lord's temple. It is, you say, your right. You are doing an act of terrible justice. But why then, so many vigorous arms to make an end of one dying man? Why these outcries? this fury? this violence? Is it thus that the people, the strong and equitable people, are wont to execute their judgments? No, no; when sure of their right, they strike their enemies, it is with the calmness of the judge, who, in freedom of soul and conscience, passes sentence. No, the strong and equitable people do not deal their blows like men blind or mad, uttering cries of rage, as if to drown the sense of some cowardly and horrible murder. No, it is not thus that they exercise the formidable right, to which you now lay claim—for you will have it—"

"Yes, we will have it!" shouted the quarryman, Ciboule, and others of the more pitiless portion of the mob; whilst a great number remained silent, struck with the words of Gabriel, who had just painted to them, in such lively colors, the frightful act they were about to commit.

"Yes," resumed the quarryman, "it is our right; we have determined to kill the poisoner!"

So saying, and with bloodshot eyes, and flushed cheek, the wretch advanced at the head of a resolute group, making a gesture as though he would have pushed aside Gabriel, who was still standing in front of the railing. But instead of resisting the bandit, the missionary advanced a couple of steps to meet him, took him by the arm, and said in a firm voice: "Come!"

And dragging, as it were, with him the stupefied quarryman, whose companions did not venture to follow at the moment, struck dumb as they were by this new incident, Gabriel rapidly traversed the space which separated him from the choir, opened the iron gate, and, still holding the quarryman by the arm, led him up to the prostrate form of Father d'Aigrigny, and said to him: "There is the victim. He is condemned. Strike!"

"I" cried the quarryman, hesitating; "I—all alone!"

"Oh!" replied Gabriel, with bitterness, "there is no danger. You can easily finish him. Look! he is broken down with suffering; he has hardly a breath of life left; he will make no resistance. Do not be afraid!"

The quarryman remained motionless, whilst the crowd, strangely impressed with this incident, approached a little nearer the railing, without daring to come within the gate.

"Strike then!" resumed Gabriel, addressing the quarryman, whilst he pointed to the crowd with a solemn gesture; "there are the judges; you are the executioner."

"No!" cried the quarryman, drawing back, and turning away his eyes; "I'm not the executioner—not I!"

The crowd remained silent. For a few moments, not a word, not a cry, disturbed the stillness of the solemn cathedral. In a desperate case, Gabriel had acted with a profound knowledge of the human heart. When the multitude, inflamed with blind rage, rushes with ferocious clamor upon a single victim, and each man strikes his blow, this dreadful species of combined murder appears less horrible to each, because they all share in the common crime; and then the shouts, the sight of blood, the desperate defence of the man they massacre, finish by producing a sort of ferocious intoxication; but, amongst all those furious madmen, who take part in the homicide, select one, and place him face to face with the victim, no longer capable of resistance, and say to him, "Strike!"—he will hardly ever dare to do so.

It was thus with the quarryman; the wretch trembled at the idea of committing a murder in cold blood, "all alone." The preceding scene had passed very rapidly; amongst the companions of the quarryman, nearest to the railing, some did not understand an impression, which they would themselves have felt as strongly as this bold man, if it had been said to them: "Do the office of executioner!" These, therefore, began to murmur aloud at his weakness. "He dares not finish the poisoner," said one.

"The coward!"

"He is afraid."

"He draws back." Hearing these words, the quarryman ran to the gate, threw it wide open, and, pointing to Father d'Aigrigny, exclaimed: "If there is one here braver than I am, let him go and finish the job—let him be, the executioner—come!"

On this proposal the murmurs ceased. A deep silence reigned once more in the cathedral. All those countenances, but now so furious, became sad, confused, almost frightened.

The deluded mob began to appreciate the ferocious cowardice of the action it had been about to commit. Not one durst go alone to strike the half expiring man. Suddenly, Father d'Aigrigny uttered a dying rattle, his head and one of his arms stirred with a convulsive movement, and then fell back upon the stones as if he had just expired.

Gabriel uttered a cry of anguish, and threw himself on his knees close to Father d'Aigrigny, exclaiming: "Great Heaven! he is dead!"

There is a singular variableness in the mind of a crowd, susceptible alike to good or evil impressions. At the heart-piercing cry of Gabriel, all these people, who, a moment before, had demanded, with loud uproar, the massacre of this man, felt touched with a sudden pity. The words: "He is dead!" circulated in low whispers through the crowd accompanied by a slight shudder, whilst Gabriel raised with one hand the victim's heavy head, and with the other sought to feel if the pulse still beat beneath the ice-cold skin.

"Mr. Curate," said the quarryman, bending towards Gabriel, "is there really no hope?"

The answer was waited for with anxiety, in the midst of deep silence. The people hardly ventured to exchange a few words in whispers.

"Blessed be God!" exclaimed Gabriel, suddenly. "His heart beats."

"His heart beats," repeated the quarryman, turning his head towards the crowd, to inform them of the good news.

"Oh! his heart beats!" repeated the others, in whispers.

"There is hope. We may yet save him," added Gabriel with an expression of indescribable happiness.

"We may yet save him," repeated the quarryman, mechanically.

"We may yet save him," muttered the crowd.

"Quick, quick," resumed Gabriel, addressing the quarryman; "help me, brother. Let us carry him to a neighboring house, where he can have immediate aid."

The quarryman obeyed with readiness. Whilst the missionary lifted Father d'Aigrigny by holding him under the arms, the quarryman took the legs of the almost inanimate body. Together, they carried him outside of the choir. At sight of the formidable quarryman, aiding the young priest to render assistance to the man whom he had just before pursued with menaces of death, the multitude felt a sudden thrill of compassion. Yielding to the powerful influence of the words and example of Gabriel, they felt themselves deeply moved, and each became anxious to offer services.

"Mr. Curate, he would perhaps be better on a chair, that one could carry upright," said Ciboule.

"Shall I go and fetch a stretcher from the hospital?" asked another.

"Mr. Curate, let me take your place; the body is too heavy for you."

"Don't trouble yourself," said a powerful man, approaching the missionary respectfully; "I can carry him alone."

"Shall I run and fetch a coach, Mr. Curate?" said a young vagabond, taking off his red cap.

"Right," said the quarryman; "run away, my buck!"

"But first, ask Mr. Curate if you are to go for a coach," said Ciboule, stopping the impatient messenger.

"True," added one of the bystanders; "we are here in a church, and Mr. Curate has the command. He is at home."

"Yes, yes; go at once, my child," said Gabriel to the obliging young vagabond.

Whilst the latter was making his way through the crowd, a voice said: "I've a little wicker-bottle of brandy; will that be of any use?"

"No doubt," answered Gabriel, hastily; "pray give it here. We can rub his temples with the spirit, and make him inhale a little."

"Pass the bottle," cried Ciboule; "but don't put your noses in it!" And, passed with caution from hand to hand, the flask reached Gabriel in safety.

Whilst waiting for the coming of the coach, Father d'Aigrigny had been seated on a chair. Whilst several good-natured people carefully supported the abbe, the missionary made him inhale a little brandy. In a few minutes, the spirit had a powerful influence on the Jesuit; he made some slight movements, and his oppressed bosom heaved with a deep sigh.

"He is saved—he will live," cried Gabriel, in a triumphant voice; "he will live, my brothers!"

"Oh! glad to hear it!" exclaimed many voices.

"Oh, yes! be glad, my brothers!" repeated Gabriel; "for, instead of being weighed down with the remorse of crime, you will have a just and charitable action to remember. Let us thank God, that he has changed your blind fury into a sentiment of compassion! Let us pray to Him, that neither you, nor those you love, may ever be exposed to such frightful danger as this unfortunate man has just escaped. Oh, my brothers!" added Gabriel, as he pointed to the image of Christ with touching emotion, which communicated itself the more easily to others from the expression of his angelic countenance; "oh, my brothers! let us never forget, that HE, who died upon that cross for the defence of the oppressed, for the obscure children of the people like to ourselves, pronounced those affectionate words so sweet to the heart; 'Love ye one another!'—Let us never forget it; let us love and help one another, and we poor people shall then become better, happier, just. Love—yes, love ye one another—and fall prostrate before that Saviour, who is the God of all that are weak, oppressed, and suffering in this world!"

So saying, Gabriel knelt down. All present respectfully followed his example, such power was there in his simple and persuasive words. At this moment, a singular incident added to the grandeur of the scene. We have said that a few seconds before the quarryman and his band entered the body of the church, several persons had fled from it. Two of these had taken refuge in the organ-loft, from which retreat they had viewed the preceding scene, themselves remaining invisible. One of these persons was a young man charged with the care of the organ, and quite musician enough to play on it. Deeply moved by the unexpected turn of an event which at first appeared so tragical, and yielding to an artistical inspiration, this young man, at the moment when he saw the people kneeling with Gabriel, could not forbear striking the notes. Then a sort of harmonious sigh, at first almost insensible, seemed to rise from the midst of this immense cathedral, like a divine aspiration. As soft and aerial as the balmy vapor of incense, it mounted and spread through the lofty arches. Little by little the faint, sweet sounds, though still as it were covered, changed to an exquisite melody, religious, melancholy, and affectionate, which rose to heaven like a song of ineffable gratitude and love. And the notes were at first so faint, so covered, that the kneeling multitude had scarcely felt surprise, and had yielded insensibly to the irresistible influence of that enchanting harmony.

Then many an eye, until now dry and ferocious, became wet with tears—many hard hearts beat gently, as they remembered the words pronounced by Gabriel with so tender an accent: "Love ye one another!" It was at this moment that Father d'Aigrigny came to himself—and opened his eyes. He thought himself under the influence of a dream. He had lost his senses in sight of a furious populace, who, with insult and blasphemy on their lips, pursued him with cries of death even to the sanctuary of the temple. He opened his eyes—and, by the pale light of the sacred lamps, to the solemn music of the organ, he saw that crowd, just now so menacing and implacable, kneeling in mute and reverential emotion, and humbly bowing their heads before the majesty of the shrine.

Some minutes after, Gabriel, carried almost in triumph on the shoulders of the crowd, entered the coach, in which Father d'Aigrigny, who by degrees had completely recovered his senses, was already reclining. By the order of the Jesuit, the coach stopped before the door of a house in the Rue de Vaugirard; he had the strength and courage to enter this dwelling alone; Gabriel was not admitted, but we shall conduct the reader thither.

CHAPTER XXVI.

THE PATIENT.

At the end of the Rue de Vaugirard, there was then a very high wall, with only one small doorway in all its length. On opening this door, you entered a yard surrounded by a railing, with screens like Venetian blinds, to prevent your seeing between the rails. Crossing this courtyard, you come to a fine large garden, symmetrically planted, at the end of which stood a building two stories high, looking perfectly comfortable, without luxury, but with all that cozy simplicity which betokens discreet opulence. A few days had elapsed since Father d'Aigrigny had been so courageously rescued by Gabriel from the popular fury. Three ecclesiastics, wearing black gowns, white bands, and square caps, were walking in the garden with a slow and measured step. The youngest seemed to be about thirty years of age; his countenance was pale, hollow, and impressed with a certain ascetic austerity. His two companions, aged between fifty or sixty, had, on the contrary, faces at once hypocritical and cunning; their round, rosy cheeks shone brightly in the sunshine, whilst their triple chins, buried in fat, descended in soft folds over the fine cambric of their bands. According to the rules of their order (they belonged to the Society of Jesus), which forbade their walking only two together, these three members of the brotherhood never quitted each other a moment.

"I fear," said one of the two, continuing a conversation already begun, and speaking of an absent person, "I fear, that the continual agitation to which the reverend father has been a prey, ever since he was attacked with the cholera, has exhausted his strength, and caused the dangerous relapse which now makes us fear for his life."

"They say," resumed the other, "that never was there seen anxiety like to his."

"And moreover," remarked the young priest, bitterly, "it is painful to think, that his reverence Father Rodin has given cause for scandal, by obstinately refusing to make a public confession, the day before yesterday when his situation appeared so desperate, that, between two fits of a delirium, it was thought right to propose to him to receive the last sacraments."

"His reverence declared that he was not so ill as they supposed," answered one of the fathers, "and that he would have the last duties performed when he thought necessary."

"The fact is, that for the last ten days, ever since he was brought here dying, his life has been, as it were, only a long and painful agony; and yet he continues to live."

"I watched by him during the first three days of his malady, with M. Rousselet, the pupil of Dr. Baleinier," resumed the youngest father; "he had hardly a moment's consciousness, and when the Lord did grant him a lucid interval, he employed it in detestable execrations against the fate which had confined him to his bed."

"It is said," resumed the other, "that Father Rodin made answer to his Eminence Cardinal Malipieri, who came to persuade him to die in an exemplary manner, worthy of a son of Loyola, our blessed founder"—at these words, the three Jesuits bowed their heads together, as if they had been all moved by the same spring—"it is said, that Father Rodin made answer to his eminence: 'I do not need to confess publicly; I WANT TO LIVE, AND I WILL LIVE.'"

"I did not hear that," said the young priest, with an indignant air; "but if Father Rodin really made use of such expressions, it is—"

Here, no doubt, reflection came to him just in time, for he stole a sidelong glance at his two silent, impassible companions, and added: "It is a great misfortune for his soul; but I am certain, his reverence has been slandered."

"It was only as a calumnious report, that I mentioned those words," said the other priest, exchanging a glance with his companion.

One of the garden gates opened, and one of the three reverend fathers exclaimed, at the sight of the personage who now entered: "Oh! here is his Eminence Cardinal Malipieri, coming to pay a visit to Father Rodin."

"May this visit of his eminence," said the young priest, calmly, "be more profitable to Father Rodin than the last!"

Cardinal Malipieri was crossing the garden, on his way to the apartment occupied by Rodin.

Cardinal Malipieri, whom we saw assisting at the sort of council held at the Princess de Saint-Dizier's, now on his way to Rodin's apartment, was dressed as a layman, but enveloped in an ample pelisse of puce-colored satin, which exhaled a strong odor of camphor, for the prelate had taken care to surround himself with all sorts of anti-cholera specifics. Having reached the second story of the house, the cardinal knocked at a little gray door. Nobody answering, he opened it, and, like a man to whom the locality was well known, passed through a sort of antechamber, and entered a room in which was a turn-up bed. On a black wood table were many phials, which had contained different medicines. The prelate's countenance seemed uneasy and morose; his complexion was still yellow and bilious; the brown circle which surrounded his black, squinting eyes appeared still darker than usual.

Pausing a moment, he looked round him almost in fear, and several times stopped to smell at his anti-cholera bottle. Then, seeing he was alone, he approached a glass over the chimney-piece, and examined with much attention the color of his tongue; after some minutes spent in this careful investigation, with the result of which he appeared tolerably satisfied, he took some preservative lozenges out of a golden box, and allowed them to melt in his mouth, whilst he closed his eyes with a sanctified air. Having taken these sanitary precautions, and again pressed his bottle to his nose, the prelate prepared to enter the third room, when he heard a tolerably loud noise through the thin partition which separated him from it, and, stopping to listen, all that was said in the next apartment easily reached his ear.

"Now that my wounds are dressed, I will get up," said weak, but sharp and imperious voice.

"Do not think of it, reverend father," was answered in a stronger tone; "it is impossible."

"You shall see if it is impossible," replied the other voice.

"But, reverend father, you will kill yourself. You are not in a state to get up. You will expose yourself to a mortal relapse. I cannot consent to it."

To these words succeeded the noise of a faint struggle, mingled with groans more angry than plaintive, and the voice resumed: "No, no, father; for your own safety, I will not leave your clothes within your reach. It is almost time for your medicine; I will go and prepare it for you."

Almost immediately after, the door opened, and the prelate saw enter a man of about twenty-five years of age, carrying on his arm an old olive great-coat and threadbare black trousers, which he threw down upon a chair.

This personage was Ange Modeste Rousselet, chief pupil of Dr. Baleinier; the countenance of the young practitioner was mild, humble, and reserved; his hair, very short in front, flowed down upon his neck behind. He made a slight start in surprise on perceiving the cardinal, and bowed twice very low, without raising his eyes.

"Before anything else," said the prelate, with his marked Italian accent, still holding to his nose his bottle of camphor, "have any choleraic symptoms returned?"

"No, my lord; the pernicious fever, which succeeded the attack of cholera, still continues."

"Very good. But will not the reverend father be reasonable? What was the noise that I just heard?"

"His reverence wished absolutely to get up and dress himself; but his weakness is so great, that he could not have taken two steps from the bed. He is devoured by impatience, and we fear that this agitation will cause a mortal relapse."

"Has Dr. Baleinier been here this morning?"

"He has just left, my lord."

"What does he think of the patient?"

"He finds him in the most alarming state, my lord. The night was so bad, that he was extremely uneasy this morning. Father Rodin is at one of those critical junctures, when a few hours may decide the life or death of the patient. Dr. Baleinier is now gone to fetch what is necessary for a very painful operation, which he is about to perform on the reverend father."

"Has Father d'Aigrigny been told of this?"

"Father d'Aigrigny is himself very unwell, as your eminence knows; he has not been able to leave his bed for the last three days."

"I inquired about him as I came up," answered the prelate, "and I shall see him directly. But, to return to Father Rodin, have you sent for his confessor, since he is in a desperate state, and about to undergo a serious operation?"

"Dr. Baleinier spoke a word to him about it, as well as about the last sacraments; but Father Rodin exclaimed, with great irritation, that they did not leave him a moment's peace, that he had as much care as any one for his salvation, and that—"

"Per Bacco! I am not thinking of him," cried the cardinal, interrupting Ange Modeste Rousselet with his pagan oath, and raising his sharp voice to a still higher key; "I am not thinking of him, but of the interests of the Company. It is indispensable that the reverend father should receive the sacraments with the most splendid solemnity, and that his end should not only be Christian, but exemplary. All the people in the house, and even strangers, should be invited to the spectacle, so that his edifying death may produce an excellent sensation."

"That is what Fathers Grison and Brunet have already endeavored to persuade his reverence, my lord; but your Eminence knows with what impatience Father Rodin received this advice, and Dr. Baleinier did not venture to persist, for fear of advancing a fatal crisis."

"Well, I will venture to do it; for in these times of revolutionary impiety, a solemnly Christian death would produce a very salutary effect on the public. It would indeed be proper to make the necessary preparations to embalm the reverend father: he might then lie in state for some days, with lighted tapers, according to Romish custom. My secretary would furnish the design for the bier; it would be very splendid and imposing; from his position in the Order, Father Rodin is entitled to have everything in the most sumptuous style. He must have at least six hundred tapers, and a dozen funeral lamps, burning spirits of wine, to hang just over the body, and light it from above: the effect would be excellent. We must also distribute little tracts to the people, concerning the pious and ascetic life of his reverence—"

Here a sudden noise, like that of some piece of metal thrown angrily on the floor, was heard from the next room, in which was the sick man, and interrupted the prelate in his description.

"I hope Father Rodin has not heard you talk of embalming him, my lord," said Rousselet, in a whisper: "his bed touches the partition, and almost everything is audible through it."

"If Father Rodin has heard me," answered the cardinal, sinking his voice, and retiring to the other end of the room, "this circumstance will enable me to enter at once on the business; but, in any case, I persist in believing that the embalming and the lying in state are required to make a good effect upon the public. The people are already frightened at the cholera, and such funeral pomp would have no small influence on the imagination."

"I would venture to observe to your Eminence, that here the laws are opposed to such exhibitions."

"The laws—already the laws!" said the cardinal, angrily; "has not Rome also her laws? And is not every priest a subject of Rome? Is it not time—"

But, not choosing, doubtless, to begin a more explicit conversation with the young doctor, the prelate resumed, "We will talk of this hereafter. But, tell me, since my last visit, has the reverend father had any fresh attacks of delirium?"

"Yes, my lord; here is the note, as your Eminence commanded." So saying Rousselet delivered a paper to the prelate. We will inform the reader that this part of the conversation between Rousselet and the cardinal was carried on at a distance from the partition, so that Rodin could hear nothing of it, whilst that which related to the embalming had been perfectly audible to him.

The cardinal, having received the note from Rousselet, perused it with an expression of lively curiosity. When he had finished, he crumpled it in his hand, and said, without attempting to dissemble his vexation, "Always nothing but incoherent expression. Not two words together, from which you can draw any reasonable conclusion. One would really think this man had the power to control himself even in his delirium, and to rave about insignificant matters only."

Then, addressing Rousselet, "You are sure that you have reported everything that escaped from him during his delirium?"

"With the exception of the same phrases, that he repeated over and over again, your Eminence may be assured that I have not omitted a single word, however unmeaning."

"Show me into Father Rodin's room," said the prelate, after a moment's silence.

"But, my lord," answered the young doctor, with some hesitation, "the fit has only left him about an hour, and the reverend father is still very weak."

"The more the reason," replied the prelate, somewhat indiscreetly. Then, recollecting himself, he added, "He will the better appreciate the consolations I have to offer. Should he be asleep, awake him, and announce my visit."

"I have only orders to receive from your Eminence," said Rousselet, bowing, and entering the next room.

Left alone, the cardinal said to himself, with a pensive air, "I always come back to that. When he was suddenly attacked by the cholera, Father Rodin believed himself poisoned by order of the Holy See. He must then have been plotting something very formidable against Rome, to entertain so abominable a fear. Can our suspicions be well founded? Is he acting secretly and powerfully on the Sacred College? But then for what end? This it has been impossible to penetrate, so faithfully has the secret been kept by his accomplices. I had hoped that, during his delirium, he would let slip some word that would put us on the trace of what we are so much interested to discover. With so restless and active a mind, delirium is often the exaggeration of some dominant idea; yet here I have the report of five different fits—and nothing—no, nothing but vague, unconnected phrases."

The return of Rousselet put an end to these reflections. "I am sorry to inform my lord that the reverend father obstinately refuses to see any one. He says that he requires absolute repose. Though very weak, he has a savage and angry look, and I should not be surprised if he overheard your Eminence talk about embalming him."

The cardinal, interrupting Rousselet, said to him, "Did Father Rodin have his last fit of delirium in the night?"

"Between three and half-past five this morning, my lord."

"Between three and half-past five," repeated the prelate, as if he wished to impress this circumstance on his memory, "the attack presented no particular symptoms?"

"No, my lord; it consisted of rambling, incoherent talk, as your Eminence may see by this note."

Then, as he perceived the prelate approaching Father Rodin's door, Rousselet added, "The reverend father will positively see no one, my lord; he requires rest, to prepare for the operation; it might be dangerous—"

Without attending to these observations, the cardinal entered Rodin's chamber. It was a tolerably large room, lighted by two windows, and simply but commodiously furnished. Two logs were burning slowly in the fireplace, in which stood a coffee-pot, a vessel containing mustard poultice, etc. On the chimney-piece were several pieces of rag, and some linen bandages. The room was full of that faint chemical odor peculiar to the chambers of the sick, mingled with so putrid a stench, that the cardinal stopped at the door a moment, before he ventured to advance further. As the three reverend fathers had mentioned in their walk, Rodin lived because he had said to himself, "I want to live, and I will live."

For, as men of timid imaginations and cowardly minds often die from the mere dread of dying, so a thousand facts prove that vigor of character and moral energy may often struggle successfully against disease, and triumph over the most desperate symptoms.

It was thus with the Jesuit. The unshaken firmness of his character, the formidable tenacity of his will (for the will has sometimes a mysterious and almost terrific power), aiding the skillful treatment of Dr. Baleinier, had saved him from the pestilence with which he had been so suddenly attacked. But the shock had been succeeded by a violent fever, which placed Rodin's life in the utmost peril. This increased danger had caused the greatest alarm to Father d'Aigrigny, who felt, in spite of his rivalry and jealousy, that Rodin was the master-spirit of the plot in which they were engaged, and could alone conduct it to a successful issue.

The curtains of the room was half closed, and admitted only a doubtful light to the bed on which Rodin was lying. The Jesuit's features had lost the greenish hue peculiar to cholera patients, but remained perfectly livid and cadaverous, and so thin, that the dry, rugged skin appeared to cling to the smallest prominence of bone. The muscles and veins of the long, lean, vulture-like neck resembled a bundle of cords. The head, covered with an old, black, filthy nightcap, from beneath which strayed a few thin, gray hairs, rested upon a dirty pillow; for Rodin would not allow them to change his linen. His iron-gray beard had not been shaved for some time, and stood out like the hairs of a brush. Under his shirt he wore an old flannel waistcoat full of holes. He had one of his arms out of bed, and his bony hairy hand, with its bluish nails, held fast a cotton handkerchief of indescribable color.

You might have taken him for a corpse, had it not been for the two brilliant sparks which still burned in the depths of his eyes. In that look, in which seemed concentrated all the remaining life and energy of the man, you might read the most restless anxiety. Sometimes his features revealed the sharpest pangs; sometimes the twisting of his hands, and his sudden starts, proclaimed his despair at being thus fettered to a bed of pain, whilst the serious interests which he had in charge required all the activity of his mind. Thus, with thoughts continually on the stretch, his mind often wandered, and he had fits of delirium, from which he woke as from a painful dream. By the prudent advice of Dr. Baleinier, who considered him not in a state to attend to matters of—importance, Father d'Aigrigny had hitherto evaded Rodin's questions with regard to the Rennepont affair, which he dreaded to see lost and ruined in consequence of his forced inaction. The silence of Father d'Aigrigny on this head, and the ignorance in which they kept him, only augmented the sick man's exasperation. Such was the moral and physical state of Rodin, when Cardinal Malipieri entered his chamber against his will.

CHAPTER XXVII.

THE LURE.

To understand fully the tortures of Rodin, reduced to inactivity by sickness, and to explain the importance of Cardinal Malipieri's visit, we must remember the audacious views of the ambitious Jesuit, who believed himself following in the steps of Sixtus V., and expected to become his equal. By the success of the Rennepont affair, to attain to the generalship of his Order, by the corruption of the Sacred College to ascend the pontifical throne, and then, by means of a change in the statutes of the Company, to incorporate the Society of Jesus with the Holy See, instead of leaving it independent, to equal and almost always rule the Papacy—such were the secret projects of Rodin.

Their possibility was sanctioned by numerous precedents, for many mere monks and priests had been suddenly raised to the pontifical dignity. And as for their morality, the accession of the Borgias, of Julius II., and other dubious Vicars of Christ, might excuse and authorize the pretensions of the Jesuits.

Though the object of his secret intrigues at Rome had hitherto been enveloped in the greatest mystery, suspicions had been excited in regard to his private communications with many members of the Sacred College. A portion of that college, Cardinal Malipieri at the head of them, had become very uneasy on the subject, and, profiting by his journey to France, the cardinal had resolved to penetrate the Jesuit's dark designs. If, in the scene we have just painted, the cardinal showed himself so obstinately bent on having a conference with Rodin, in spite of the refusal of the latter, it was because the prelate hoped, as we shall soon see, to get by cunning at the secret, which had hitherto been so well concealed. It was, therefore, in the midst of all these extraordinary circumstances, that Rodin saw himself the victim of a malady, which paralyzed his strength, at the moment when he had need of all his activity, and of all the resources of his mind. After remaining for some seconds motionless near the door, the cardinal, still holding his bottle under his nose, slowly approached the bed where Rodin lay.

The latter, enraged at this perseverance, and wishing to avoid an interview which for many reasons was singularly odious to him, turned his face towards the wall, and pretended to be asleep. Caring little for this feint, and determined to profit by Rodin's state of weakness, the prelate took a chair, and, conquering his repugnance, sat down close to the Jesuit's bed.

"My reverend and very dear father, how do you find yourself?" said he to him, in a honeyed tone, which his Italian accent seemed to render still more hypocritical. Rodin pretended not to hear, breathed hard, and made no answer. But the cardinal, not without disgust, shook with his gloved hand the arm of the Jesuit, and repeated in a louder voice: "My reverend and very dear father, answer me, I conjure you!"

Rodin could not restrain a movement of angry impatience, but he continued silent. The cardinal was not a man to be discouraged by so little; he again shook the arm of the Jesuit, somewhat more roughly, repeating, with a passionless tenacity that would have incensed the most patient person in the world: "My reverend and very dear father, since you are not asleep, listen to me, I entreat of you."

Irritable with pain, exasperated by the obstinacy of the prelate, Rodin abruptly turned his head, fixed on the Roman his hollow eyes, shining with lurid fire, and, with lips contracted by a sardonic smile, said to him, bitterly: "You must be very anxious, my lord, to see me embalmed, and lie in state with tapers, as you were saying just now, for you thus to come to torment me in my last moments, and hasten my end!"

"Oh, my good father! how can you talk so?" cried the cardinal, raising his hands as if to call heaven to witness to the sincerity of the tender interest he felt for the Jesuit.

"I tell you that I heard all just now, my lord; for the partition is thin," added Rodin, with redoubled bitterness.

"If you mean that, from the bottom of my soul, I desired that you should make an exemplary and Christian end, you are perfectly right, my dear father. I did say so; for, after a life so well employed, it would be sweet to see you an object of adoration for the faithful!"

"I tell you, my lord," cried Rodin, in a weak and broken voice, "that it is ferocious to express such wishes in the presence of a dying man. Yes," he added, with growing animation, that contrasted strongly with his weakness, "take care what you do; for if I am too much plagued and pestered—if I am not allowed to breathe my last breath quietly—I give you notice that you will force me to die in anything but a Christian manner, and if you mean to profit by an edifying spectacle, you will be deceived."

This burst of anger having greatly fatigued Rodin, his head fell back upon the pillow, and he wiped his cracked and bleeding lips with his old cotton handkerchief.

"Come, come, be calm, my very dear father," resumed the cardinal, with a patronizing air; "do not give way to such gloomy ideas. Doubtless,

Providence reserves you for great designs, since you have been already delivered from so much peril. Let us hope that you will be likewise saved from your present danger."

Rodin answered by a hoarse growl, and turned his face towards the wall.

The imperturbable prelate continued: "The views of Providence are not confined to your salvation, my very dear father. Its power has been manifested in another way. What I am about to tell you is of the highest importance. Listen attentively."

Without turning his head, Rodin muttered in a tone of angry bitterness, which betrayed his intense sufferings: "They desire my death. My chest is on fire, my head racked with pain, and they have no pity. Oh, I suffer the tortures of the damned!"

"What! already" thought the Roman, with a smile of sarcastic malice; then he said aloud: "Let me persuade you, my very dear father—make an effort to listen to me; you will not regret it."

Still stretched upon the bed, Rodin lifted his hands clasped upon his cotton handkerchief with a gesture of despair, and then let them fall again by his side.

The cardinal slightly shrugged his shoulders, and laid great stress on what follows, so that Rodin might not lose a word of it: "My dear father, it has pleased Providence that, during your fit of raving, you have made, without knowing it, the most important revelations."

The prelate waited with anxious curiosity for the effect of the pious trap he had laid for the Jesuit's weakened faculties. But the latter, still turned towards the wall, did not appear to have heard him and remained silent.

"You are, no doubt, reflecting on my words, my dear father," resumed the cardinal; "you are right, for it concerns a very serious affair. I repeat to you that Providence has allowed you, during your delirium, to betray your most secret thoughts—happily, to me alone. They are such as would compromise you in the highest degree. In short, during your delirium of last night, which lasted nearly two hours, you unveiled the secret objects of your intrigues at Rome with many of the members of the Sacred College."

The cardinal, rising softly, stooped over the bed to watch the expression of Rodin's countenance. But the latter did not give him time. As a galvanized corpse starts into strange and sudden motion, Rodin sprang into a sitting posture at the last words of the prelate.

"He has betrayed himself," said the cardinal, in a low voice, in Italian. Then, resuming his seat, he fixed on the Jesuit his eyes, that sparkled with triumphant joy.

Though he did not hear the exclamation of Malipieri, nor remark the expression of his countenance, Rodin, notwithstanding his state of weakness, instantly felt the imprudence of his start. He pressed his hand to his forehead, as though he had been seized with a giddiness; then, looking wildly round him, he pressed to his trembling lips his old cotton handkerchief, and gnawed it mechanically for some seconds.

"Your emotion and alarm confirm the sad discoveries I have made," resumed the cardinal, still more rejoicing at the success of his trick; "and now, my dear father," added he, "you will understand that it is for your best interest to enter into the most minute detail as to your projects and accomplices at Rome. You may then hope, my dear father, for the indulgence of the Holy See—that is, if your avowals are sufficiently explicit to fill up the chasms necessarily left in a confession made during delirium."

Rodin, recovered from his first surprise, perceived, but too late, that he had fallen into a snare, not by any words he had spoken, but by his too significant movements. In fact, the Jesuit had feared for a moment that he might have betrayed himself during his delirium, when he heard himself accused of dark intrigues with Rome; but, after some minutes of reflection, his common sense suggested: "If this crafty Roman knew my secret, he would take care not to tell me so. He has only suspicions, confirmed by my involuntary start just now."

Rodin wiped the cold sweat from his burning forehead. The emotion of this scene augmented his sufferings, and aggravated the danger of his condition. Worn out with fatigue, he could not remain long in a sitting posture, and soon fell back upon the bed.

"Per Bacco!" said the cardinal to himself, alarmed at the expression of the Jesuit's face; "if he were to die before he had spoken, and so escape the snare!"

Then, leaning over the bed, the prelate asked: "What is the matter, my very dear father?"

"I am weak, my lord—I am in pain—I cannot express what I suffer."

"Let us hope, my very dear father, that this crisis will have no fatal results; but the contrary may happen, and it behooves the salvation of your soul to make instantly the fullest confession. Were it even to exhaust your strength, what is this perishable body compared to eternal life?"

"Of what confession do you speak, my lord?" said Rodin, in a feeble and yet sarcastic tone.

"What confession!" cried the amazed cardinal; "why, with regard to your dangerous intrigues at Rome."

"What intrigues?" asked Rodin.

"The intrigues you revealed during your delirium," replied the prelate, with still more angry impatience. "Were not your avowals sufficiently explicit? Why, then, this culpable hesitation to complete them?"

"My avowals—were explicit—you assure me?" said Rodin, pausing after each word for want of breath, but without losing his energy and presence of mind.

"Yes, I repeat it," resumed the cardinal; "with the exception of a few chasms, they were most explicit."

"Then why repeat them?" said Rodin, with the same sardonic smile on his violet lips.

"Why repeat them?" cried the angry prelate. "In order to gain pardon; for if there is indulgence and mercy for the repentant sinner, there must be condemnation and curses for the hardened criminal!"

"Oh, what torture! I am dying by slow fire!" murmured Rodin. "Since I have told all," he resumed, "I have nothing more to tell. You know it already."

"I know all—doubtless, I know all," replied the prelate, in a voice of thunder; "but how have I learned it? By confessions made in a state of unconsciousness. Do you think they will avail you anything? No; the moment is solemn—death is at hand, tremble to die with a sacrilegious falsehood on your lips," cried the prelate, shaking Rodin violently by the arm; "dread the eternal flames, if you dare deny what you know to be the truth. Do you deny it?"

"I deny nothing," murmured Rodin, with difficulty. "Only leave me alone!"

"Then heaven inspires you," said the cardinal, with a sigh of satisfaction; and, thinking he had nearly attained his object, he resumed, "Listen to the divine word, that will guide you, father. You deny nothing?"

"I was—delirious—and cannot—(oh! how I suffer!)" added Rodin, by way of parenthesis; "and cannot therefore—deny—the nonsense—I may have uttered!"

"But when this nonsense agrees with the truth," cried the prelate, furious at being again deceived in his expectation; "but when raving is an involuntary, providential revelation—"

"Cardinal Malipieri—your craft is no match—for my agony," answered Rodin, in a failing voice. "The proof—that I have not told my secret—if I have a secret—is—that you want to make me tell it!" In spite of his pain and weakness, the Jesuit had courage to raise himself in the bed, and look the cardinal full in the face, with a smile of bitter irony. After which he fell back on the pillow, and pressed his hands to his chest, with a long sigh of anguish.

"Damnation! the infernal Jesuit has found me out!" said the cardinal to himself, as he stamped his foot with rage. "He sees that he was compromised by his first movement; he is now upon his guard; I shall get nothing more from him—unless indeed, profiting by the state of weakness in which he is, I can, by entreaties, by threats, by terror—"

The prelate was unable to finish. The door opened abruptly, and Father d'Aigrigny entered the room, exclaiming with an explosion of joy: "Excellent news!"

CHAPTER XXVIII.

GOOD NEWS.

By the alteration in the countenance of Father d'Aigrigny, his pale cheek, and the feebleness of his walk, one might see that the terrible scene in the square of Notre-Dame, had violently reacted upon his health. Yet his face was radiant and triumphant, as he entered Rodin's chamber, exclaiming: "Excellent news!"

On these words, Rodin started. In spite of his weakness, he raised his head, and his eyes shone with a curious, uneasy, piercing expression. With his lean hand, he beckoned Father d'Aigrigny to approach the bed, and said to him, in a broken voice, so weak that it was scarcely audible: "I am very ill—the cardinal has nearly finished me—but if this excellent news—relates to the Rennepont affair—of which I hear nothing—it might save me yet!"

"Be saved then!" cried Father d'Aigrigny, forgetting the recommendations of Dr. Baleinier; "read, rejoice! What you foretold is beginning to be realized!"

So saying, he drew a paper from his pocket, and delivered it to Rodin, who seized it with an eager and trembling hand. Some minutes before, Rodin would have been really incapable of continuing his conversation with the cardinal, even if prudence had allowed him to do so; nor could he have read a single line, so dim had his sight become. But, at the words of Father d'Aigrigny, he felt such a renewal of hope and vigor, that, by a mighty effort of energy and will, he rose to a sitting posture, and, with clear head, and look of intelligent animation, he read rapidly the paper that Father d'Aigrigny had just delivered to him.

The cardinal, amazed at this sudden transfiguration, asked himself if he beheld the same man, who, a few minutes before, had fallen back on his bed, almost insensible. Hardly had Rodin finished reading, than he uttered a cry of stifled joy, saying, with an accent impossible to describe: "ONE gone! it works—'tis well!" And, closing his eyes in a kind of ecstatic transport, a smile of proud triumph overspread his face, and rendered him still more hideous, by discovering his yellow and gumless teeth. His emotion was so violent, that the paper fell from his trembling hand.

"He has fainted," cried Father d'Aigrigny, with uneasiness, as he leaned over Rodin. "It is my fault, I forgot that the doctor cautioned me not to talk to him of serious matters."

"No; do not reproach yourself," said Rodin, in a low voice, half-raising himself in the bed. "This unexpected joy may perhaps cure me. Yes—I scarce know what I feel—but look at my cheeks—it seems to me, that, for the first time since I have been stretched on this bed of pain, they are a little warm."

Rodin spoke the truth. A slight color appeared suddenly on his livid and icy cheeks; his voice though still very weak, became less tremulous, and he exclaimed, in a tone of conviction that startled Father d'Aigrigny and the prelate, "This first success answers for the others. I read the future. Yes, yes; our cause will triumph. Every member of the execrable Rennepont family will be crushed—and that soon you will see—"

Then, pausing, Rodin threw himself back on the pillow, exclaiming: "Oh! I am choked with joy. My voice fails me."

"But what is it?" asked the cardinal of Father d'Aigrigny.

The latter replied, in a tone of hypocritical sanctity: "One of the heirs of the Rennepont family, a poor fellow, worn out with excesses and debauchery, died three days ago, at the close of some abominable orgies, in which he had braved the cholera with sacrilegious impiety. In consequence of the indisposition that kept me at home, and of another circumstance, I only received to-day the certificate of the death of this victim of intemperance and irreligion. I must proclaim it to the praise of his reverence"—pointing to Rodin—"that he told me, the worst enemies of the descendants of that infamous renegade would be their own bad passions, and that the might look to them as our allies against the whole impious race. And so it has happened with Jacques Rennepont."

"You see," said Rodin, in so faint a voice that it was almost unintelligible, "the punishment begins already. One of the Renneponts is dead—and believe me—this certificate," and he pointed to the paper that Father d'Aigrigny held in his hand, "will one day be worth forty millions to the Society of Jesus—and that—because—"

The lips alone finished the sentence. During some seconds, Rodin's voice had become so faint, that it was at last quite imperceptible. His larynx, contracted by violent emotion, no longer emitted any sound. The Jesuit, far from being disconcerted by this incident, finished his phrase, as it were, by expressive pantomime. Raising his head proudly he tapped his forehead with his forefinger, as if to express that it was to his ability this first success was owing. But he soon fell back again on the bed, exhausted, breathless, sinking, with his cotton handkerchief pressed once more to his parched lips. The good news, as Father d'Aigrigny called it, had not cured Rodin. For a moment only, he had had the courage to forget his pain. But the slight color on his cheek soon disappeared; his face became once more livid. His sufferings, suspended for a moment, were so much increased in violence, that he writhed beneath the coverlet, and buried his face in the pillow, extending his arms above his head, and holding them stiff as bars of iron. After this crisis, intense as it was rapid: during which Father d'Aigrigny and the prelate bent anxiously over him, Rodin, whose face was bathed in cold sweat, made a sign that he suffered less, and that he wished to drink of a potion to which he pointed. Father d'Aigrigny fetched it for him, and while the cardinal held him up with marked disgust, the abbe administered a few spoonfuls of the potion, which almost immediately produced a soothing effect.

"Shall I call M. Rousselet?" said Father d'Aigrigny, when Rodin was once more laid down in bed.

Rodin shook his head; then, with a fresh effort, he raised his right hand, opened it, and pointed with his forefinger to a desk in a corner of the room, to signify that, being no longer able to speak, he wished to write.

"I understand your reverence," said Father d'Aigrigny; "but first calm yourself. Presently, if you require it. I will give you writing materials."

Two knocks at the outer door of the next room interrupted this scene. From motives of prudence, Father d'Aigrigny had begged Rousselet to remain in the first of the three rooms. He now went to open the door, and Rousselet handed him a voluminous packet, saying: "I beg pardon for disturbing you, father, but I was told to let you have these papers instantly."

"Thank you, M. Rousselet," said Father d'Aigrigny; "do you know at what hour Dr. Baleinier will return?"

"He will not be long, father, for he wishes to perform before night the painful operation, that will have a decisive effect on the condition of Father Rodin. I am preparing what is necessary for it," added Rousselet, as he pointed to a singular and formidable apparatus, which Father d'Aigrigny examined with a kind of terror.

"I do not know if the symptom is a serious one," said the Jesuit; "but the reverend father has suddenly lost his voice."

"It is the third time this has happened within the last week," said Rousselet; "the operation of Dr. Baleinier will act both on the larynx and on the lungs."

"Is the operation a very painful one?" asked Father d'Aigrigny.

"There is, perhaps, none more cruel in surgery," answered the young doctor; "and Dr. Baleinier has partly concealed its nature from Father Rodin."

"Please to wait here for Dr. Baleinier, and send him to us as soon as he arrives," resumed Father d'Aigrigny: and, returning to the sick chamber, he sat down by the bedside, and said to Rodin, as he showed him the letter: "Here are different reports with regard to different members of the Rennepont family, whom I have had looked after by others, my indisposition having kept me at home for the last few days. I do not know, father, if the state of your health will permit you to hear—"

Rodin made a gesture, at once so supplicating and peremptory, that Father d'Aigrigny felt there would be at least as much danger in refusing as in granting his request; so, turning towards the cardinal, still inconsolable at not having discovered the Jesuit's secret, he said to him with respectful deference, pointing at the same time to the letter: "Have I the permission of your Eminence?"

The prelate bowed, and replied: "Your affairs are ours, my dear father. The Church must always rejoice in what rejoices your glorious Company."

Father d'Aigrigny unsealed the packet, and found in it different notes in different handwritings. When he had read the first, his countenance darkened, and he said, in a grave tone: "A misfortune—a great misfortune."

Rodin turned his head abruptly, and looked at him with an air of uneasy questioning.

"Florine is dead of the cholera," answered Father d'Aigrigny; "and what is the worst," added he, crumpling the note between his hands, "before dying, the miserable creature confessed to Mdlle. de Cardoville that she long acted as a spy under the orders of your reverence."

No doubt the death of Florine, and the confession she had made, crossed some of the plans of Rodin, for he uttered an inarticulate murmur, and his countenance expressed great vexation.

Passing to another note, Father d'Aigrigny continued: "This relates to Marshal Simon, and is not absolutely bad, but still far from satisfactory, as it announces some amelioration in his position. We shall see if it merits belief, by information from another source."

Rodin made a sign of impatience, to hasten Father d'Aigrigny to read the note, which he did as follows. "'For some days, the mind of the marshal has appeared to be less sorrowful, anxious and agitated. He lately passed two hours with his daughters, which had not been the case for some time before. The harsh countenance of the soldier Dagobert is becoming smoother—a sure sign of some amelioration in the condition of the marshal. Detected by their handwriting, the last anonymous letters were returned by Dagobert to the postman, without having been opened by the marshal. Some other method must be found to get them delivered.'"

Looking at Rodin, Father d'Aigrigny said to him: "Your reverence thinks with me that this note is not very satisfactory?"

Rodin held down his head. One saw by the expression of his countenance how much he suffered by not being able to speak. Twice he put his hand to his throat, and looked at Father d'Aigrigny with anguish.

"Oh!" cried Father d'Aigrigny, angrily, when he had perused another note, "for one lucky chance, to-day brings some very black ones."

At these words turning hastily to Father d'Aigrigny, and extending his trembling hands, Rodin questioned him with look and gesture. The cardinal, sharing his uneasiness, exclaimed: "What do you learn by this note, my dear father?"

"We thought the residence of M. Hardy in our house completely unknown," replied Father d'Aigrigny, "but we now fear that Agricola Baudoin has discovered the retreat of his old master, and that he has even communicated with him by letter, through a servant of the house. So," added the reverend father, angrily, "during the three days that I have not been able to visit the pavilion, one of my servants must have been bought over. There is one of them, a man blind of one eye, whom I have always suspected—the wretch! But no: I will not yet believe this treachery. The consequences would be too deplorable; for I know how matters stand, and that such a correspondence might ruin everything. By awaking in M. Hardy memories with difficulty laid asleep, they might destroy in a single day all that has been done since he inhabits our house. Luckily, this note contains only doubts and fears; my other information will be more positive, and will not, I hope, confirm them."

"My dear father," said the cardinal, "do not despair. The Lord will not abandon the good cause!"

Father d'Aigrigny seemed very little consoled by this assurance. He remained still and thoughtful, whilst Rodin writhed his head in a paroxysm of mute rage, as he reflected on this new check.

"Let us turn to the last note," said Father d'Aigrigny, after a moment of thoughtful silence. "I have so much confidence in the person who sends it, that I cannot doubt the correctness of the information it contains. May it contradict the others!"

In order not to break the chain of facts contained in this last note, which was to have so startling an effect on the actors in this scene, we shall leave it to the reader's imagination to supply the exclamations of surprise, hate, rage and fear of Father d'Aigrigny, and the terrific pantomime of Rodin, during the perusal of this formidable document, the result of the observations of a faithful and secret agent of the reverend fathers. Comparing this note with the other information received, the results appeared more distressing to the reverend fathers. Thus Gabriel had long and frequent conferences with Adrienne, who before was unknown to him. Agricola Baudoin had opened a communication with Francis Hardy, and the officers of justice were on the track of the authors and instigators of the riot which had led to the burning of the factory of Baron Tripeaud's rival. It seemed almost certain that Mdlle. de Cardoville had had an interview with Prince Djalma.

This combination of facts showed that, faithful to the threats she had uttered to Rodin, when she had unmasked the double perfidy of the reverend father, Mdlle. de Cardoville was actively engaged in uniting the scattered members of her family, to form a league against those dangerous enemies, whose detestable projects, once unveiled and boldly encountered, could hardly have a chance of success. The reader will now understand the tremendous effect of this note on Father d'Aigrigny and Rodin—on Rodin, stretched powerless on a bed of pain at the moment when the scaffolding, raised with so much labor, seemed to be tumbling around him.

CHAPTER XXIX.

THE OPERATION.

We have given up the attempt to paint the countenance, attitude, and gesticulation of Rodin during the reading of this note, which seemed to ruin all his most cherished hopes. Everything was failing at once, at the moment when only superhuman trust in the success of his plans could give him sufficient energy to strive against mortal sickness. A single, absorbing thought had agitated him even to delirium: What progress, during his illness, had been made in this immense affair? He had first heard a good piece of news, the death of Jacques Rennepont; but now the advantages of this decease, which reduced the number of the heirs from seven to six, were entirely lost. To what purpose would be this death, if the other members of the family, dispersed and persecuted with such infernal perseverance, were to unite and discover the enemies who had so long aimed at them in darkness? If all those wounded hearts were to console, enlighten, support each other, their cause would be gained, and the inheritance rescued from the reverend fathers. What was to be done?

Strange power of the human will!—Rodin had one foot in the grave, he was almost at the last gasp; his voice had failed him. And yet that obstinate nature, so full of energy and resources, did not despair. Let but a miracle restore his health, and that firm confidence in the success of his projects which has given him power to struggle against disease, tells him that he could yet save all—but then he must have health and life! Health! life! His physician does not know if he will survive the shock—if he can bear the pain—of a terrible operation. Health! life! and just now Rodin heard talk of the solemn funeral they had prepared for him. And yet—health, life, he will have them. Yes; he has willed to live—and he has lived—why should he not live longer? He will live—because he has willed it.

All that we have just written passed though Rodin's mind in a second. His features, convulsed by the mental torment he endured, must have assumed a very strange expression, for Father d'Aigrigny and the cardinal looked at him in silent consternation. Once resolved to live, and to sustain a desperate struggle with the Rennepont family, Rodin acted in consequence. For a few moments Father d'Aigrigny and the prelate believed themselves under the influence of a dream. By an effort of unparalleled energy, and as if moved by hidden mechanism, Rodin sprang from the bed, dragging the sheet with him, and trailing it, like a shroud, behind his livid and fleshless body. The room was cold; the face of the Jesuit was bathed in sweat; his naked and bony feet left their moist print upon the stones.

"What are you doing? It is death!" cried Father d'Aigrigny, rushing towards Rodin, to force him to lie down again.

But the latter, extending one of his skeleton arms, as hard as iron, pushed aside Father d'Aigrigny with inconceivable vigor, considering the state of exhaustion in which he had so long been.

"He has the strength of a man in a fit of epilepsy," said Father d'Aigrigny, recovering his balance.

With a steady step Rodin advanced to the desk on which Dr. Baleinier daily wrote his prescriptions. Seating himself before it, the Jesuit took pen and paper, and began to write in a firm hand. His calm, slow, and sure movements had in them something of the deliberateness remarked in somnambulists. Mute and motionless, hardly knowing whether they dreamed or not, the cardinal and Father d'Aigrigny remained staring at the incredible coolness of Rodin, who, half-naked, continued to write with perfect tranquillity.

"But, father," said the Abbe d'Aigrigny, advancing towards him, "this is madness!"

Rodin shrugged his shoulders, stopped him with a gesture and made him a sign to read what he had just written.

The reverend father expected to see the ravings of a diseased brain; but he took the note, whilst Rodin commenced another.

"My lord," exclaimed Father d'Aigrigny, "read this!"

The cardinal read the paper, and returning it to the reverend father with equal amazement, added: "It is full of reason, ability, and resources. We shall thus be able to neutralize the dangerous combination of Abbe Gabriel and Mdlle. de Cardoville, who appear to be the most formidable leaders of the coalition."

"It is really miraculous," said Father d'Aigrigny.

"Oh, my dear father!" whispered the cardinal, shaking his head; "what a pity that we are the only witnesses of this scene! What an excellent MIRACLE we could have made of it! In one sense, it is another Raising of Lazarus!"

"What an idea, my lord!" answered Father d'Aigrigny, in a low voice. "It is perfect—and we must not give it up—"

This innocent little plot was interrupted by Rodin, who, turning his head, made a sign to Father d'Aigrigny to approach, and delivered to him another sheet, with this note attached: "To be executed within an hour."

Having rapidly perused the paper, Father d'Aigrigny exclaimed: "Right! I had not thought of that. Instead of being fatal, the correspondence between Agricola and M. Hardy may thus have the best results. Really," added the reverend father in a low voice to the prelate, while Rodin continued to write, "I am quite confounded. I read—I see—and yet I can hardly believe my eyes. Just before, exhausted and dying—and now with his mind as clear and penetrating as ever. Can this be one of the phenomena of somnambulism, in which the mind alone governs and sustains the body?"

Suddenly the door opened, and Dr. Baleinier entered the room. At sight of Rodin, seated half-naked at the desk, with his feet upon the cold stones, the doctor exclaimed, in a tone of reproach and alarm: "But, my lord—but, father—it is murder to let the unhappy man do this!—If he is delirious from fever, he must have the strait-waistcoat, and be tied down in bed."

So saying. Dr. Baleinier hastily approached Rodin, and took him by the arm. Instead of finding the skin dry and chilly, as he expected, he found it flexible, almost damp. Struck with surprise, the doctor sought to feel the pulse of the left hand, which Rodin resigned, to him, whilst he continued working with the right.

"What a prodigy!" cried the doctor, as he counted Rodin's pulse; "for a week past, and even this morning, the pulse has been abrupt, intermittent, almost insensible, and now it is firm, regular—I am really puzzled—what then has happened? I can hardly believe what I see," added the doctor, turning towards Father d'Aigrigny and the cardinal.

"The reverend father, who had first lost his voice, was next seized with such furious and violent despair caused by the receipt of bad news," answered Father d'Aigrigny, "that we feared a moment for his life; while now, on the contrary, the reverend father has gained sufficient strength to go to his desk, and write for some minutes, with a clearness of argument and expression, which has confounded both the cardinal and myself."

"There is no longer any doubt of it," cried the doctor. "The violent despair has caused a degree of emotion, which will admirably prepare the reactive crisis, that I am now almost certain of producing by the operation."

"You persist in the operation?" whispered Father d'Aigrigny, whilst Rodin continued to write.

"I might have hesitated this morning; but, disposed as he now is for it, I must profit by the moment of excitement, which will be followed by greater depression."

"Then, without the operation—" said the cardinal.

"This fortunate and unexpected crisis will soon be over, and the reaction may kill him, my lord."

"Have you informed him of the serious nature of the operation?"

"Pretty nearly, my lord."

"But it is time to bring him to the point."

"That is what I will do, my lord," said Dr. Baleinier; and approaching Rodin, who continued to write, he thus addressed him, in a firm voice: "My reverend father, do you wish to be up and well in a week?"

Rodin nodded, full of confidence, as much as to say: "I am up already."

"Do not deceive yourself," replied the doctor. "This crisis is excellent, but it will not last, and if we would profit by it, we must proceed with the operation of which I have spoken to you—or, I tell you plainly, I answer for nothing after such a shock."

Rodin was the more struck with these words, as, half an hour ago, he had experienced the short duration of the improvement occasioned by Father d'Aigrigny's good news, and as already he felt increased oppression on the chest.

Dr. Baleinier, wishing to decide him, added: "In a word, father, will you live or die?"

Rodin wrote rapidly this answer, which he gave to the doctor: "To live, I would let you cut me limb from limb. I am ready for anything." And he made a movement to rise.

"I must tell you, reverend father, so as not to take you by surprise," added Dr. Baleinier, "that this operation is cruelly painful."

Rodin shrugged his shoulders and wrote with a firm hand: "Leave me my head; you may take all the rest."

The doctor read these words aloud, and the cardinal and Father d'Aigrigny looked at each other in admiration of this dauntless courage.

"Reverend father," said Dr. Baleinier, "you must lie down."

Rodin wrote: "Get everything ready. I have still some orders to write. Let me know when it is time."

Then folding up a paper, which he had sealed with a wafer, Rodin gave these words to Father d'Aigrigny: "Send this note instantly to the agent who addressed the anonymous letters to Marshal Simon."

"Instantly, reverend father," replied the abbe; "I will employ a sure messenger."

"Reverend father," said Baleinier to Rodin, "since you must write, lie down in bed, and write there, during our little preparations."

Rodin made an affirmative gesture, and rose. But already the prognostics of the doctor were realized. The Jesuit could hardly remain standing for a second; he fell back into a chair, and looked at Dr. Baleinier with anguish, whilst his breathing became more and more difficult.

The doctor said to him: "Do not be uneasy. But we must make haste. Lean upon me and Father d'Aigrigny."

Aided by these two supporters, Rodin was able to regain the bed. Once there, he made signs that they should bring him pen, ink, and paper. Then he continued to write upon his knees, pausing from time to time, to breathe with great difficulty.

"Reverend father," said Baleinier to d'Aigrigny, "are you capable of acting as one of my assistants in the operation? Have you that sort of courage?"

"No," said the reverend father; "in the army I could never assist at an amputation. The sight of blood is too much for me."

"There will be no blood," said the doctor, "but it will be worse. Please send me three of our reverend fathers to assist me, and ask M. Rousselet to bring in the apparatus."

Father d'Aigrigny went out. The prelate approached the doctor, and whispered, pointing to Rodin: "Is he out of danger?"

"If he stands the operation—yes, my lord."

"Are you sure that he can stand it?"

"To him I should say 'yes,' to you 'I hope so.'"

"And were he to die, would there be time to administer the sacraments in public, with a certain pomp, which always causes some little delay?"

"His dying may continue, my lord—a quarter of an hour."

"It is short, but we must be satisfied with that," said the prelate.

And, going to one of the windows, he began to tap with his fingers on the glass, while he thought of the illumination effects, in the event of Rodin's lying in state. At this moment, Rousselet entered, with a large square box under his arm. He placed it on the drawers, and began to arrange his apparatus.

"How many have you prepared?" said the doctor.

"Six, sir."

"Four will do, but it is well to be fully provided. The cotton is not too thick?"

"Look, sir."

"Very good."

"And how is the reverend father?" asked the pupil.

"Humph!" answered the doctor, in a whisper. "The chest is terribly clogged, the respiration hissing, the voice gone—still there is a change."

"All my fear is, sir, that the reverend father will not be able to stand the dreadful pain."

"It is another chance; but, under the circumstances, we must risk all. Come, my dear boy, light the—taper; I hear our assistants."

Just then Father d'Aigrigny entered the room, accompanied by the three Jesuits, who, in the morning, had walked in the garden. The two old men, with their rosy cheeks, and the young one, with the ascetic countenance, all three dressed in black, with their square caps and white bands, appeared perfectly ready to assist Dr. Baleinier in his formidable operation.

CHAPTER XXX.

THE TORTURE.

"Reverend fathers," said Dr. Baleinier, graciously, to the three, "I thank you for your kind aid. What you have to do is very simple, and, by the blessing of heaven, this operation will save the life of our dear Father Rodin."

The three black-gowns cast up their eyes piously, and then bowed altogether, like one man. Rodin, indifferent to what was passing around him, never ceased an instant to write or reflect. Nevertheless, in spite of his apparent calmness, he felt such difficulty in breathing, that more than once Dr. Baleinier had turned round uneasily, as he heard the stifled rattling in the throat of the sick man. Making a sign to his pupil, the doctor approached Rodin and said to him: "Come, reverend father; this is the important moment. Courage!"

No sign of alarm was expressed in the Jesuit's countenance. His features remained impassible as those of a corpse. Only, his little reptile eyes sparkled still more brightly in their dark cavities. For a moment, he looked round at the spectators of this scene; then, taking his pen between his teeth, he folded and wafered another letter, placed it on the table beside the bed, and nodded to Dr. Baleinier, as if to say: "I am ready."

"You must take off your flannel waistcoat, and your shirt, father." Rodin hesitated an instant, and the doctor resumed: "It is absolutely necessary, father."

Aided by Baleinier, Rodin obeyed, whilst the doctor added, no doubt to spare his modesty: "We shall only require the chest, right and left, my dear father."

And now, Rodin, stretched upon his back, with his dirty night-cap still on his head, exposed the upper part of a livid trunk, or rather, the bony cage of a skeleton, for the shadows of the ribs and cartilages encircled the skin with deep, black lines. As for the arms, they resembled bones twisted with cord and covered with tanned parchment.

"Come, M. Rousselet, the apparatus!" said Baleinier.

Then addressing the three Jesuits, he added: "Please draw near, gentlemen; what you have to do is very simple, as you will see."

It was indeed very simple. The doctor gave to each of his four assistants a sort of little steel tripod about two inches in diameter and three in height; the circular centre of this tripod was filled with cotton; the instrument was held in the left hand by means of a wooden handle. In the right hand each assistant held a small tin tube about eighteen inches long; at one end was a mouthpiece to receive the lips of the operator, and the other spread out so as to form a cover to the little tripod. These preparations had nothing alarming in them. Father d'Aigrigny and the prelate, who looked on from a little distance, could not understand how this operation should be so painful. They soon understood it.

Dr. Baleinier, having thus provided his four assistants, made them approach Rodin, whose bed had been rolled into the middle of the room. Two of them were placed on one side, two on the other.

"Now, gentlemen," said Dr. Baleinier, "set light to the cotton; place the lighted part on the skin of his reverence, by means of the tripod which contains the wick; cover the tripod with the broad part of the tube, and then blow through the other end to keep up the fire. It is very simple, as you see."

It was, in fact, full of the most patriarchal and primitive ingenuity. Four lighted cotton rocks, so disposed as to burn very slowly, were applied to the two sides of Rodin's chest. This is vulgarly called the moxa. The trick is done, when the whole thickness of the skin has been burnt slowly through. It lasts seven or eight minutes. They say that an amputation is nothing to it. Rodin had watched the preparations with intrepid curiosity. But, at the first touch of the four fires, he writhed like a serpent, without being able to utter a cry. Even the expression of pain was denied him. The four assistants being disturbed by, the sudden start of Rodin, it was necessary to begin again.

"Courage, my dear father! offer these sufferings to the Lord!" said Dr. Baleinier, in a sanctified tone. "I told you the operation would be very painful; but then it is salutary in proportion. Come; you that have shown such decisive resolution, do not fail at the last movement!"

Rodin had closed his eyes, conquered by the first agony of pain. He now opened them, and looked at the doctor as if ashamed of such weakness. And yet on the sides of his chest were four large, bleeding wounds—so violent had been the first singe. As he again extended himself on the bed of torture, Rodin made a sign that he wished to write. The doctor gave him the pen, and he wrote as follows, by way of memorandum; "It is better not to lose any time. Inform Baron Tripeaud of the warrant issued against Leonard, so that he may be on his guard."

Having written this note, the Jesuit gave it to Dr. Baleinier, to hand it to Father d'Aigrigny, who was as much amazed as the doctor and the cardinal, at such extraordinary presence of mind in the midst of such horrible pain.

Rodin, with his eyes fixed on the reverend father, seemed to wait with impatience for him to leave the room to execute his orders. Guessing the thought of Rodin, the doctor whispered Father d'Aigrigny, who went out.

"Come, reverend father," said the doctor, "we must begin again. This time do not move."

Rodin did not answer, but clasped his hands over his head, closed his eyes, and presented his chest. It was a strange, lugubrious, almost fantastic spectacle. The three priests, in their long black gowns, leaned over this body, which almost resembled a corpse, and blowing through their tubes into the chest of the patient, seemed as if pumping up his blood by some magic charm. A sickening odor of burnt flesh began to spread through the silent chamber, and each assistant heard a slight crackling beneath the smoking trivet; it was the skin of Rodin giving way to the action of fire, and splitting open in four different parts of his chest. The sweat poured from his livid face, which it made to shine; a few locks of his gray hair stood up stiff and moist from his temples. Sometimes the spasms were so violent, that the veins swelled on his stiffened arms, and were stretched like cords ready to break.

Enduring this frightful torture with as much intrepid resignation as the savage whose glory consists in despising pain, Rodin gathered his strength and courage from the hope—we had almost said the certainty—of life. Such was the make of this dauntless character, such the energy of this powerful mind, that, in the midst of indescribable torments, his one fixed idea never left him. During the rare intervals of suffering—for pain is equal even at this degree of intensity—Rodin still thought of the Rennepont inheritance, and calculated his chances, and combined his measures, feeling that he had not a minute to lose. Dr. Baleinier watched him with extreme attention, waiting for the effects of the reaction of pain upon the patient, who seemed already to breathe with less difficulty.

Suddenly Rodin placed his hand on his forehead, as if struck with some new idea, and turning his head towards Dr. Baleinier, made a sign to him to suspend the operation.

"I must tell you, reverend father," answered the doctor, "that it is not half finished, and, if we leave off, the renewal will be more painful—"

Rodin made a sign that he did not care, and that he wanted to write.

"Gentlemen, stop a moment," said Dr. Baleinier; "keep down your moxas, but do not blow the fire."

So the fire was to burn slowly, instead of fiercely, but still upon the skin of the patient. In spite of this pain, less intense, but still sharp and keen,

Rodin, stretched upon his back, began to write, holding the paper above his head. On the first sheet he traced some alphabetic signs, part of a cipher known to himself alone. In the midst of the torture, a luminous idea had crossed his mind; fearful of forgetting it amidst his sufferings, he now took note of it. On another paper he wrote the following, which was instantly delivered to Father d'Aigrigny: "Send B. immediately to Faringhea, for the report of the last few days with regard to Djalma, and let B. bring it hither on the instant." Father d'Aigrigny went out to execute this new order. The cardinal approached a little nearer to the scene of the operation, for, in spite of the bad odor of the room, he took delight in seeing the Jesuit half roasted, having long cherished against him the rancor of an Italian and a priest.

"Come, reverend father," said the doctor to Rodin, "continue to be admirably courageous, and your chest will free itself. You have still a bitter moment to go through—and then I have good hope."

The patient resumed his former position. The moment Father d'Aigrigny returned, Rodin questioned him with a look, to which the reverend father replied by a nod. At a sign from the doctor, the four assistants began to blow through the tubes with all their might. This increase of torture was so horrible, that, in spite of his self-control, Rodin gnashed his teeth, started convulsively, and so expanded his palpitating chest, that, after a violent spasm, there rose from his throat and lungs a scream of terrific pain—but it was free, loud, sonorous.

"The chest is free!" cried the doctor, in triumph. "The lungs have play—the voice returns—he is saved!—Blow, gentlemen, blow; and, reverend father, cry out as much as you please: I shall be delighted to hear you, for it will give you relief. Courage! I answer for the result. It is a wonderful cure. I will publish it by sound of trumpet."

"Allow me, doctor," whispered Father d'Aigrigny, as he approached Dr. Baleinier; "the cardinal can witness, that I claimed beforehand the publication of this affair—as a miraculous fact."

"Let it be miraculous then," answered Dr. Baleinier, disappointed—for he set some value on his own work.

On hearing he was saved, Rodin though his sufferings were perhaps worse than ever, for the fire had now pierced the scarf-skin, assumed almost an infernal beauty. Through the painful contraction of his features shone the pride of savage triumph; the monster felt that he was becoming once more strong and powerful, and he seemed conscious the evils that his fatal resurrection was to cause. And so, of still writhing beneath the flames, he pronounced these words, the first that struggled from his chest: "I told you I should live!"

"You told us true," cried the doctor, feeling his pulse; "the circulation is now full and regular, the lungs are free. The reaction is complete. You are saved."

At this moment, the last shreds of cotton had burnt out. The trivets were withdrawn, and on the skeleton trunk of Rodin were seen four large round blisters. The skin still smoked, and the raw flesh was visible beneath. In one of his sudden movements, a lamp had been misplaced, and one of these burns was larger than the other, presenting as it were to the eye a double circle. Rodin looked down upon his wounds. After some seconds of silent contemplation, a strange smile curled his lips. Without changing his position, he glanced at Father d'Aigrigny with an expression impossible to describe, and said to him, as he slowly counted the wounds touching them with his flat and dirty nail: "Father d'Aigrigny, what an omen!—Look here! one Rennepont—two Renneponts—three Renneponts—four Renneponts—where is then the fifth!—Ah! here—this wound will count for two. They are twins."[41] And he emitted a little dry, bitter laugh. Father d'Aigrigny, the cardinal, and Dr. Baleinier, alone understood the sense of these mysterious and fatal words, which Rodin soon completed by a terrible allusion, as he exclaimed, with prophetic voice, and almost inspired air: "Yes, I say it. The impious race will be reduced to ashes, like the fragments of this poor flesh. I say it, and it will be so. I said I would live—and I do live!"

[41] Jacques Rennepont being dead, and Gabriel out of the field, in consequence of his donation, there remained only five persons of the family—Rose and Blanche, Djalma, Adrienne, and Hardy.

CHAPTER XXXI.

VICE AND VIRTUE.

Two days have elapsed since Rodin was miraculously restored to life. The reader will not have forgotten the house in the Rue Clovis, where the reverend father had an apartment, and where also was the lodging of Philemon, inhabited by Rose-Pompon. It is about three o'clock in the afternoon. A bright ray of light, penetrating through a round hole in the door Mother Arsene's subterraneous shop, forms a striking contrast with the darkness of this cavern. The ray streams full upon a melancholy object. In the midst of fagots and faded vegetables, and close to a great heap of charcoal, stands a wretched bed; beneath the sheet, which covers it, can be traced the stiff and angular proportions of a corpse. It is the body of Mother Arsene herself, who died two days before, of the cholera. The burials have been so numerous, that there has been no time to remove her remains. The Rue Clovis is almost deserted. A mournful silence reigns without, often broken by the sharp whistling of the north wind. Between the squalls, one hears a sort of pattering. It is the noise of the large rats, running to and fro across the heap of charcoal.

Suddenly, another sound is heard, and these unclean animals fly to hide themselves in their holes. Some one is trying to force open the door, which communicates between the shop and the passage. It offers but little resistance, and, in a few seconds, the worn-out lock gives way, and a woman enters. For a short time she stands motionless in the obscurity of the damp and icy cave. After a minute's hesitation, the woman advances and the ray of light illumines the features of the Bacchanal Queen. Slowly, she approached the funeral couch. Since the death of Jacques, the alteration in the countenance of Cephyse had gone on increasing. Fearfully pale, with her fine black hair in disorder, her legs and feet naked, she was barely covered with an old patched petticoat and a very ragged handkerchief.

When she came near the bed, she cast a glance of almost savage assurance at the shroud. Suddenly she drew back, with a low cry of involuntary terror. The sheet moved with a rapid undulation, extending from the feet to the head of the corpse. But soon the sight of a rat, flying along the side of the worm-eaten bedstead, explained the movement of the shroud. Recovering from her fright, Cephyse began to look for several things, and collected them in haste, as though she dreaded being surprised in the miserable shop. First, she seized a basket, and filled it with charcoal; then, looking from side to side, she discovered in a corner an earthen pot, which she took with a burst of ominous joy.

"It is not all, it is not all," said Cephyse, as she continued to search with an unquiet air.

At last she perceived near the stove a little tin box, containing flint, steel and matches. She placed these articles on the top of the basket, and took it in one hand, and the earthen pot in the other. As she passed near the corpse of the poor charcoal-dealer, Cephyse said, with a strange smile: "I rob you, poor Mother Arsene, but my theft will not do me much good."

Cephyse left the shop, reclosed the door as well as she could, went up the passage, and crossed the little court-yard which separated the front of the building from that part in which Rodin had lodged. With the exception of the windows of Philemon's apartment, where Rose-Pompon had so often sat perched like a bird, warbling Beranger, the other windows of the house were open. There had been deaths on the first and second floors, and, like many others, they were waiting for the cart piled up with coffins.

The Bacchanal Queen gained the stairs, which led to the chambers formerly occupied by Rodin. Arrived at the landing-place she ascended another ruinous staircase, steep as a ladder, and with nothing but an old rope for a rail. She at length reached the half-rotten door of a garret, situated in the roof. The house was in such a state of dilapidation, that, in many places the roof gave admission to the rain, and allowed it to penetrate into this cell, which was not above ten feet square, and lighted by an attic window. All the furniture consisted of an old straw mattress, laid upon the ground, with the straw peeping out from a rent in its ticking; a small earthenware pitcher, with the spout broken, and containing a little water, stood by the side of this couch. Dressed in rags, Mother Bunch was seated on the side of the mattress, with her elbows on her knees, and her face concealed in her thin, white hands. When Cephyse entered the room, the adopted sister of Agricola raised her head; her pale, mild face seemed thinner than ever, hollow with suffering, grief, misery; her eyes, red with weeping, were fixed on her sister with an expression of mournful tenderness.

"I have what we want, sister," said Cephyse, in a low, deep voice; "in this basket there is wherewith to finish our misery."

Then, showing to Mother Bunch the articles she had just placed on the floor, she added: "For the first time in my life, I have been a thief. It made me ashamed and frightened; I was never intended for that or worse. It is a pity." added she, with a sardonic smile.

After a moment's silence, the hunchback said to her sister, in a heart rending tone: "Cephyse—my dear Cephyse—are you quite determined to die?"

"How should I hesitate?" answered Cephyse, in a firm voice. "Come, sister, let us once more make our reckoning. If even I could forget my shame, and Jacques' contempt in his last moments, what would remain to me? Two courses only: first, to be honest, and work for my living. But you know that, in spite of the best will in the world, work will often fail, as it has failed for the last few days, and, even when I got it, I would have to live on four to five francs a week. Live? that is to say, die by inches. I know that already, and I prefer dying at once. The other course would be to live a life of infamy—and that I will not do. Frankly, sister, between frightful misery, infamy, or death, can the choice be doubtful? Answer me!"

Then, without giving Mother Bunch time to speak, Cephyse added, in an abrupt tone: "Besides, what is the good of discussing it? I have made up my mind, and nothing shall prevent my purpose, since all that you, dear sister, could obtain from me, was a delay of a few days, to see if the cholera would not save us the trouble. To please you I consented; the cholera has come, killed every one else in the house, but left us. You see, it is better to do one's own business," added she, again smiling bitterly. Then she resumed: "Besides, dear sister, you also wish to finish with life."

"It is true, Cephyse," answered the sempstress, who seemed very much depressed; "but alone—one has only to answer for one's self—and to die with you," added she, shuddering, "appears like being an accomplice in your death."

"Do you wish, then, to make an end of it, I in one place, you in another?— that would be agreeable!" said Cephyse, displaying in that terrible moment the sort of bitter and despairing irony which is more frequent than may be imagined in the midst of mortal anguish.

"Oh, no, no!" said the other in alarm, "not alone—I will not die alone!"

"Do you not see, dear sister, we are right not to part? And yet," added Cephyse, in a voice of emotion, "my heart almost breaks sometimes, to think that you will die like me."

"How selfish!" said the hunchback, with a faint smile. "What reasons have I to love life? What void shall I leave behind me?"

"But you are a martyr, sister," resumed Cephyse. "The priests talk of saints! Is there one of them so good as you? And yet you are about to die like me, who have always been idle, careless, sinful—while you were so hardworking, so devoted to all who suffered. What should I say? You were an angel on the earth; and yet you will die like me, who have fallen as low as a woman can fall," added the unfortunate, casting down her eyes.

"It is strange," answered Mother Bunch, thoughtfully. "Starting from the same point, we have followed different roads, and yet we have reached the same goal—disgust of life. For you, my poor sister, but a few days ago, life was so fair, so full of pleasure and of youth; and now it is equally heavy with us both. After all, I have followed to the end what was my duty," added she, mildly. "Agricola no longer needs me. He is married; he loves, and is beloved; his happiness is secured. Mdlle. de Cardoville wants for nothing. Fair, rich, prosperous—what could a poor creature like myself do for her? Those who have been kind to me are happy. What prevents my going now to my rest? I am so weary!"

"Poor sister!" said Cephyse, with touching emotion, which seemed to expand her contracted features; "when I think that, without informing me, and in spite of your resolution never to see that generous young lady, who protected you, you yet had the courage to drag yourself to her house, dying with fatigue and want, to try to interest her in my fate—yes, dying, for your strength failed on the Champs-Elysees."

"And when I was able to reach the mansion, Mdlle. de Cardoville was unfortunately absent—very unfortunately!" repeated the hunchback, as she looked at Cephyse with anguish; "for the next day, seeing that our last resource had failed us, thinking more of me than of yourself, and determined at any price to procure us bread—"

She could not finish. She buried her face in her hands, and shuddered.

"Well, I did as so many other hapless women have done when work fails or wages do not suffice, and hunger becomes too pressing," replied Cephyse, in a broken voice; "only that, unlike so many others, instead of living on my shame, I shall die of it."

"Alas! this terrible shame which kills you, my poor Cephyse, because you have a heart, would have been averted, had I seen Mdlle. de Cardoville, or had she but answered the letter which I asked leave to write to her at the porter's lodge. But her silence proves to me that she is justly hurt at my abrupt departure from her house. I can understand it; she believes me guilty of the blackest ingratitude—for she must have been greatly offended not to have deigned to answer me—and therefore I had not the courage to write a second time. It would have been useless, I am sure; for, good and just as she is, her refusals are inexorable when she believes them deserved. And besides, for what good? It was too late; you had resolved to die!"

"Oh, yes, quite resolved: for my infamy was gnawing at my heart. Jacques had died in my arms despising me; and I loved him—mark me, sister," added Cephyse, with passionate enthusiasm, "I loved him as we love only once in life!"

"Let our fate be accomplished, then!" said Mother Bunch with a pensive air.

"But you have never told me, sister, the cause of your departure from Mdlle. de Cardoville's," resumed Cephyse, after a moment's silence.

"It will be the only secret that I shall take with me, dear Cephyse," said the other, casting down her eyes. And she thought, with bitter joy, that she would soon be delivered from the fear which had poisoned the last days of her sad life—the fear of meeting Agricola, informed of the fatal and ridiculous love she felt for him.

For, it must be said, this fatal and despairing love was one of the causes of the suicide of the unfortunate creature. Since the disappearance of her journal, she believed that the blacksmith knew the melancholy secret contained in its sad pages. She doubted not the generosity and good heart of Agricola; but she had such doubts of herself, she was so ashamed of this passion, however pure and noble, that, even in the extremity to which Cephyse and herself were reduced—wanting work, wanting bread—no power on earth could have induced her to meet Agricola, in an attempt to ask him for assistance. Doubtless, she would have taken another view of the subject if her mind had not been obscured by that sort of dizziness to which the firmest characters are exposed when their misfortunes surpass all bounds. Misery, hunger, the influence, almost contagious in such a moment, of the suicidal ideas of Cephyse, and weariness of a life so long devoted to pain and mortification, gave the last blow to the sewing-girl's reason. After long struggling against the fatal design of her sister, the poor, dejected, broken-hearted creature finished by determining to share Cephyse's fate, and seek in death the end of so many evils.

"Of what are you thinking, sister?" said Cephyse, astonished at the long silence. The other replied, trembling: "I think of that which made me leave Mdlle. de Cardoville so abruptly, and appear so ungrateful in her eyes. May the fatality which drove me from her house have made no other victims! may my devoted service, however obscure and powerless, never be missed by her, who extended her noble hand to the poor sempstress, and deigned to call me sister! May she be happy—oh, ever happy!" said Mother Bunch, clasping her hands with the ardor of a sincere invocation.

"That is noble, sister—such a wish in such a moment!" said Cephyse.

"Oh," said her sister, with energy, "I loved, I admired that marvel of genius, and heart, and ideal beauty—I viewed her with pious respect—for never was the power of the Divinity revealed in a more adorable and purer creation. At least one of my last thoughts will have been of her."

"Yes, you will have loved and respected your generous patroness to the last."

"To the last!" said the poor girl, after a moment's silence. "It is true—you are right—it will soon be the last!—in a few moments, all will be finished. See how calmly we can talk of that which frightens so many others!"

"Sister, we are calm because we are resolved."

"Quite resolved, Cephyse," said the hunchback, casting once more a deep and penetrating glance upon her sister.

"Oh, yes, if you are only as determined as I am."

"Be satisfied; if I put off from day to day the final moment," answered the sempstress, "it was because I wished to give you time to reflect. As for me—"

She did not finish, but she shook her head with an air of the utmost despondency.

"Well, sister, let us kiss each other," said Cephyse; "and, courage!"

The hunchback rose, and threw herself into her sister's arms. They held one another fast in a long embrace. There followed a few seconds of deep and solemn silence, only interrupted by the sobs of the sisters, for now they had begun to weep.

"Oh, heaven! to love each other so, and to part forever!" said Cephyse. "It is a cruel fate."

"To part?" cried Mother Bunch, and her pale, mild countenance, bathed in tears, was suddenly illumined with a ray of divine hope; "to part, sister? oh, no! What makes me so calm is the deep and certain expectation, which I feel here at my heart, of that better world where a better life awaits us. God, so great, so merciful, so prodigal of good, cannot destine His creatures to be forever miserable. Selfish men may pervert His benevolent designs, and reduce their brethren to a state of suffering and despair. Let us pity the wicked and leave them! Come up on high, sister; men are nothing there, where God is all. We shall do well there. Let us depart, for it is late."

So saying, she pointed to the ruddy beams of the setting sun, which began to shine upon the window.

Carried away by the religious enthusiasm of her sister, whose countenance, transfigured, as it were, by the hope of an approaching deliverance, gleamed brightly in the reflected sunset, Cephyse took her hands, and, looking at her with deep emotion, exclaimed, "Oh, sister! how beautiful you look now!"

"Then my beauty comes rather late in the day," said Mother Bunch, with a sad smile.

"No, sister; for you appear so happy, that the last scruples I had upon your account are quite gone."

"Then let us make haste," said the hunchback, as she pointed to the chafing-dish.

"Be satisfied, sister—it will not be long," said Cephyse. And she took the chafing-dish full of charcoal, which she had placed in a corner of the garret, and brought it out into the middle of the room.

"Do you know how to manage it?" asked the sewing-girl approaching.

"Oh! it is very simple," answered Cephyse; "we have only to close the door and window, and light the charcoal."

"Yes, sister; but I think I have heard that every opening must be well stopped, so as to admit no current of air."

"You are right, and the door shuts so badly."

"And look at the holes in the roof."

"What is to be done, sister?"

"I will tell you," said Mother Bunch. "The straw of our mattress, well twisted, will answer every purpose."

"Certainly," replied Cephyse. "We will keep a little to light our fire, and with the rest we will stop up all the crevices in the roof, and make filling for our doors and windows."

Then, smiling with that bitter irony, so frequent, we repeat, in the most gloomy moments, Cephyse added, "I say, sister, weather-boards at our doors and windows, to prevent the air from getting in—what a luxury! we are as delicate as rich people."

"At such a time, we may as well try to make ourselves a little comfortable," said Mother Bunch, trying to jest like the Bacchanal Queen.

And with incredible coolness, the two began to twist the straw into lengths of braid, small enough to be stuffed into the cracks of the door, and also constructed large plugs, destined to stop up the crevices in the roof. While this mournful occupation lasted, there was no departure from the calm and sad resignation of the two unfortunate creatures.

CHAPTER XXXII.

SUICIDE.

Cephyse and her sister continued with calmness the preparations for their death.

Alas! how many poor young girls, like these sisters, have been, and still will be, fatally driven to seek in suicide a refuge from despair, from infamy, or from a too miserable existence! And upon society will rest the terrible responsibility of these sad deaths, so long as thousands of human creatures, unable to live upon the mockery of wages granted to their labor, have to choose between these three gulfs of shame and woe; a life of enervating toil and mortal privations, causes of premature death; prostitution, which kills also, but slowly—by contempt, brutality, and uncleanness; suicide—which kills at once.

In a few minutes, the two sisters had constructed, with the straw of their couch, the calkings necessary to intercept the air, and to render suffocation more expeditious and certain.

The hunchback said to her sister, "You are the taller, Cephyse, and must look to the ceiling; I will take care of the window and door."

"Be satisfied, sister; I shall have finished before you," answered Cephyse.

And the two began carefully to stop up every crevice through which a current of air could penetrate into the ruined garret. Thanks to her tall stature, Cephyse was able to reach the holes in the roof, and to close them up entirely. When they had finished this sad work, the sisters again approached, and looked at each other in silence.

The fatal moment drew near; their faces, though still calm, seemed slightly agitated by that strange excitement which always accompanies a double suicide.

"Now," said Mother Bunch, "now for the fire!"

She knelt down before the little chafing-dish, filled with charcoal. But Cephyse took hold of her under the arm, and obliged her to rise again, saying to her, "Let me light the fire—that is my business."

"But, Cephyse—"

"You know, poor sister, that the smell of charcoal gives you the headache!"

At the simplicity of this speech, for the Bacchanal Queen had spoken seriously, the sisters could not forbear smiling sadly.

"Never mind," resumed Cephyse; "why suffer more and sooner than is necessary?"

Then, pointing to the mattress, which still contained a little straw, Cephyse added, "Lie down there, good little sister; when our fire is alight, I will come and sit down by you."

"Do not be long, Cephyse."

"In five minutes it will be done."

The tall building, which faced the street, was separated by a narrow court from that which contained the retreat of the two sisters, and was so much higher, that when the sun had once disappeared behind its lofty roof, the garret soon became dark. The light, passing through the dirty panes of the small window, fell faintly on the blue and white patchwork of the old mattress, on which Mother Bunch was now stretched, covered with rags. Leaning on her left arm, with her chin resting in the palm of her hand, she looked after her sister with an expression of heart-rending grief. Cephyse, kneeling over the chafing-dish, with her face close to the black charcoal, above which already played a little bluish flame, exerted herself to blow the newly-kindled fire, which was reflected on the pale countenance of the unhappy girl.

The silence was deep. No sound was heard but the panting breath of Cephyse, and, at intervals, the slight crackling of the charcoal, which began to burn, and already sent forth a faint sickening vapor. Cephyse, seeing the fire completely lighted, and feeling already a little dizzy, rose from the ground, and said to her sister, as she approached her, "It is done!"

"Sister," answered Mother Bunch, kneeling on the mattress, whilst Cephyse remained standing, "how shall we place ourselves? I should like to be near you to the last."

"Stop!" said Cephyse, half executing the measures of which she spoke, "I will sit on the mattress with my back against the wall. Now, little sister, you lie there. Lean your head upon my knees, and give me your hand. Are you comfortable so?"

"Yes—but I cannot see you."

"That is better. It seems there is a moment—very short, it is true—in which one suffers a good deal. And," added Cephyse, in a voice of emotion, "it will be as well not to see each other suffer."

"You are right, Cephyse."

"Let me kiss that beautiful hair for the last time," said Cephyse, as she pressed her lips to the silky locks which crowned the hunchback's pale and melancholy countenance, "and then—we will remain very quiet."

"Sister, your hand," said the sewing-girl; "for the last time, your hand—and then, as you say, we will move no more. We shall not have to wait long, I think, for I begin to feel dizzy. And you, sister?"

"Not yet," replied Cephyse; "I only perceive the smell of the charcoal."

"Do you know where they will bury us?" said Mother Bunch, after a moment's silence.

"No. Why do you ask?"

"Because I should like it to be in Pere-la-Chaise. I went there once with Agricola and his mother. What a fine view there is!—and then the trees, the flowers, the marble—do you know the dead are better lodged—than the living—and—"

"What is the matter, sister?" said Cephyse to her companion, who had stopped short, after speaking in a slow voice.

"I am giddy—my temples throb," was the answer. "How do you feel?"

"I only begin to be a little faint; it is strange—the effect is slower with me than you."

"Oh! you see," said Mother Bunch, trying to smile, "I was always so forward. At school, do you remember, they said I was before the others. And, now it happens again."

"I hope soon to overtake you this time," said Cephyse.

What astonished the sisters was quite natural. Though weakened by sorrow and misery, the Bacchanal Queen, with a constitution as robust as the other was frail and delicate, was necessarily longer than her sister in feeling the effects of the deleterious vapor. After a moment's silence, Cephyse resumed, as she laid her hand on the head she still held upon her knees, "You say nothing, sister! You suffer, is it not so?"

"No," said Mother Bunch, in a weak voice; "my eyelids are heavy as lead—I am getting benumbed—I feel that I speak more slowly—but I have no acute pain. And you, sister?"

"Whilst you were speaking, I felt giddy—and now my temples throb violently."

"As it was with me just now. One would think it was more painful and difficult to die."

Then after a moment's silence, the hunchback said suddenly to her sister, "Do you think that Agricola will much regret me, and think of me for some time?"

"How can you ask?" said Cephyse, in a tone of reproach.

"You are right," answered Mother Bunch, mildly; "there is a bad feeling in such a doubt—but if you knew—"

"What, sister?"

The other hesitated for an instant, and then said, dejectedly, "Nothing." Afterwards, she added, "Fortunately, I die convinced that he will never miss me. He married a charming girl, who loves him, I am sure, and will make him perfectly happy."

As she pronounced these last words, the speaker's voice grew fainter and fainter. Suddenly she started and said to Cephyse, in a trembling, almost frightened tone, "Sister! Hold me in your arms—I am afraid—everything looks dark—everything is turning round." And the unfortunate girl, raising herself a little, hid her face in her sister's bosom, and threw his weak arms around her.

"Courage, sister!" said Cephyse, in a voice which was also growing faint, as she pressed her closer to her bosom; "it will soon be over."

And Cephyse added, with a kind of envy, "Oh! why does my sister's strength fail so much sooner than mine? I have still my perfect senses and I suffer less than she does. Oh! if I thought she would die first!—But, no—I will go and hold my face over the chafing-dish rather."

At the movement Cephyse made to rise, a feeble pressure from her sister held her back. "You suffer, my poor child!" said Cephyse, trembling.

"Oh yes! a good deal now—do not leave me!"

"And I scarcely at all," said Cephyse, gazing wildly at the chafing-dish. "Ah!" added she, with a kind of fatal! joy; "now I begin to feel it—I choke—my head is ready to split."

And indeed the destructive gas now filled the little chamber, from which it had, by degrees, driven all the air fit for respiration. The day was closing in, and the gloomy garret was only lighted by the reflection of the burning charcoal, which threw a red glare on the sisters, locked in each other's arms. Suddenly Mother Bunch made some slight convulsive movements, and pronounced these words in a failing voice: "Agricola—Mademoiselle de Cardoville—Oh! farewell!—Agricola—I—"

Then she murmured some unintelligible words; the convulsive moments ceased, and her arms, which had been clasped round Cephyse, fell inert upon the mattress.

"Sister!" cried Cephyse, in alarm, as she raised Mother Bunch's head, to look at her face. "Not already, sister!—And I?—and I?"

The sewing-girl's mild countenance was not paler than usual. Only her eyes, half-closed, seemed no longer to see anything, and a half-smile of mingled grief and goodness lingered an instant about her violet lips, from which stole the almost imperceptible breath—and then the mouth became motionless, and the face assumed a great serenity of expression.

"But you must not die before me!" cried Cephyse, in a heart-rending tone, as she covered with kisses the cold cheek. "Wait for me, sister! wait for me!"

Mother Bunch did not answer. The head, which Cephyse let slip from her hands, fell back gently on the mattress.

"My God. It is not my fault, if we do not die together!" cried Cephyse in despair, as she knelt beside the couch, on which the other lay motionless.

"Dead!" she murmured in terror. "Dead before me!—Perhaps it is that I am the strongest. Ah! it begins—fortunately—like her, I see everything dark-blue—I suffer—what happiness!—I can scarcely breathe. Sister!" she added, as she threw her arms round her loved one's neck; "I am coming—I am here!"

At the same instant the sound of footsteps and voices was heard from the staircase. Cephyse had still presence of mind enough to distinguish the sound. Stretched beside the body of her sister, she raised her head hastily.

The noise approached, and a voice was heard exclaiming, not far from the doer: "Good heavens! what a smell of fire!"

And, at the same instant, the door was violently shaken, and another voice exclaimed: "Open! open!"

"They will come in—they will save me—and my sister is dead—Oh, no! I will not have the baseness to survive her!"

Such was the last thought of Cephyse. Using what little strength she had left, she ran to the window and opened it—and, at the same instant that the half-broken door yielded to a vigorous effort from without, the unfortunate creature precipitated herself from that third story into the court below. Just then, Adrienne and Agricola appeared on the threshold of the chamber. In spite of the stifling odor of the charcoal, Mdlle. de Cardoville rushed into the garret, and, seeing the stove, she exclaimed, "The unhappy girl has killed herself!"

"No, she has thrown herself from the window," cried Agricola: for, at the moment of breaking open the door, he had seen a human form disappear in that direction, and he now ran to the window.

"Oh! this is frightful!" he exclaimed, with a cry of horror, as he put his hand before his eyes, and returned pale and terrified to Mdlle. de Cardoville.

But, misunderstanding the cause of his terror, Adrienne, who had just perceived Mother Bunch through the darkness, hastened to answer: "No! she is here."

And she pointed to the pale form stretched on the mattress, beside which Adrienne now threw herself on her knees. Grasping the hands of the poor sempstress, she found them as cold as ice. Laying her hand on her heart, she could not feel it beat. Yet, in a few seconds, as the fresh air rushed into the room from the door and window, Adrienne thought she remarked an almost imperceptible pulsation, and she exclaimed: "Her heart beats! Run quickly for help! Luckily, I have my smelling bottle."

"Yes, yes! help for her—and for the other too, if it is yet time!" cried the smith in despair, as he rushed down the stairs, leaving Mdlle. de Cardoville still kneeling by the side of the mattress.

This book has been considered important throughout the human history, and so that this work is never forgotten we have made efforts in its preservation by republishing this book in a modern format for present and future generations. This whole book has been reformatted, retyped and designed. These books are not made of scanned copies of their original work and hence the text is clear and readable.

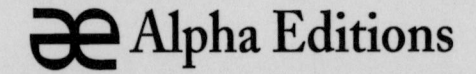

Alpha Editions

ISBN 978-93-6299-306-9